MW00328804

LIBERTY OR LOVE!

Atlas Anti-Classic 16

Robert Desnos

Liberty or Love!
&
Mourning for Mourning

Translated and Introduced by Terry Hale

ATLAS PRESS LONDON 2012

Published by Atlas Press
BCM ATLAS PRESS, LONDON WC1N 3XX
©Éditions Gallimard, Paris, 1962
English edition ©2012 Atlas Press
A CIP catalogue for this book is available from
The British Library
ISBN: 1 900565 45 5
ISBN-13: 978-1-900565-45-5
Printed and bound by CPI, Chippenham.
USA distribution: Artbook/DAP
155 Sixth Avenue, 2nd Floor,
New York, NY 10013
www.artbook.com
UK distribution: TURNAROUND
www.turnaround-uk.com

Contents

Introduction

"At the present epoch, in the intellectual domain," wrote André Breton in an article published in July 1924, "there are to my knowledge three fanatics of the first magnitude: Picasso, Freud and Desnos. The latter, however, is infinitely further than the other two from having said his last word. ... Symbolism, Cubism and Dada have long since run their course. *Surrealism* is the order of the day and Desnos is its prophet."[1]

Breton is equally flattering elsewhere. "It is Desnos more than any of us who has come closest to the Surrealist truth," he proclaimed towards the end of 1924 in the *First Manifesto of Surrealism*. Furthermore, it is Desnos "who, in his still unpublished works and in the course of the numerous experiments to which he has been a party, has fully justified the hope I placed in Surrealism and leads me to believe that a great deal more will still come of it. Desnos *speaks Surrealism at will*."[2]

André Breton's testimony is all the more extraordinary if one stops to consider that at the moment he made these remarks Robert Desnos had indeed published very little — nothing more, in fact, than a few accounts of dreams and a couple of short automatic texts. These had almost all appeared in *Littérature* — the review founded by Breton, Aragon and Soupault five years earlier — between 1922 and June 1924. Even *Deuil pour Deuil* (translated here as *Mourning for Mourning*), a selection of Desnos's automatic texts produced while in a trance-like state, although dated 1924 would not seem to have been available in the bookshops until December of that year at the earliest. *La Liberté ou l'amour! [Liberty or Love!]*, frequently considered Desnos's masterpiece, would not be published until 1927, nearly three years later. Even then, the latter had — at the insistence of the authorities (and for reasons we shall explain in a moment) — to be almost immediately withdrawn from circulation. It would not be available again, and then only in a highly expurgated form, for at least another year — by which time the author's formal rupture with the Surrealist movement was close at hand.

Two questions, therefore, need to be addressed here: whether Breton, hyperbole apart, was broadly correct in his original assessment of Desnos's talents and, if so, whether *Liberty or Love!* lives up to his expectations.

It was some time towards the end of 1919 that Breton and Louis Aragon decided that the Certà, a bar in the Passage de l'Opéra, should become the meeting place for themselves and their friends. And it was here, at the invitation of Benjamin Péret, that fifteen months or so later, in the spring of 1921, Desnos met Breton, Aragon, Tristan Tzara, Jacques Rigaut and Georges Ribemont-Dessaignes for the first time. The meeting was not a success. Péret bungled the introductions so that the ice was never broken. Desnos was still in uniform, which seemed to make a bad impression. Breton, Péret, Tzara and Desnos none the less dined at a nearby restaurant. Desnos was twenty, four years younger than Breton or Tzara, and remained tongue-tied throughout the meal. "I imagine that I left the impression that particular evening of being a perfect imbecile," he remarked later. It was not important. Desnos was sent to Morocco on active service shortly afterwards, and it was only on his return to Paris, after his demobilisation in March 1922, that he cemented ties with those he had passed such an immemorable evening with the year before.[3]

It was also around 1919 that Breton first began to become interested in those "more or less incomplete sentences which at the onset of sleep, when one is quite alone, the mind is able to perceive, although it is impossible to say where they have come from."[4] Many such phrases seemed startling enough to warrant further study. One which occurred to Breton about this time — unfortunately he did not note it down immediately — ran something like this: "There is a man cut in two by the window." This phrase, says Breton, was accompanied by the faint visual image of a walking man truncated at the waist by a window perpendicular to the axis of his body: "No doubt about it, what was involved was the simple righting in space of a man leaning out of a window. But this window having followed the man's shift of position, I realised that I was dealing with an image of a rather rare type which I decided to incorporate into my stock of poetic construction."[5]

Freud, whose work was still largely unknown in France at this time, had already described numerous visual puns of this kind which, he claimed, are frequently to be encountered in dreams. But if Freud sought to explain the psychological significance of such phenomena, it fell to the Surrealists to harness their potential in the creative domain. During the late spring and early summer of 1919, Breton and Philippe Soupault filled entire notebooks with spontaneously irrupting automatic phrases. Out of these sessions — the results of which varied according to the rapidity of composition — sprang the first characteristically Surrealist 'novel': *The Magnetic Fields*.

The authors, however, claimed no more for this work than that it represented a first step towards a much wider attempt to liberate the unconscious from the fetters which bound it. Further investigations would encompass, besides much else, the use of hypnotic states, the simulation of mental illness, prolonged discussion as to the nature of human sexuality, and eventually even embrace sociological or ethnological research of the kind undertaken, for example, by Michel Leiris. In 1922, the year of Desnos's return to France, much of this still lay in the future. "We know, up to a certain point, what we understand, my friends and I, by Surrealism," wrote Breton hesitantly in the November 1922 issue of *Littérature*. "This word, which we did not invent and which we could easily have allowed to become part of the most general critical vocabulary, is employed by us in a precise sense. By it we have agreed to designate a certain psychic automatism which corresponds closely to the dream state, a state which it is still extremely difficult to define."[6] It was in the course of those further experiments, undertaken to refine this new concept of *psychic* automatism, that Desnos distinguished himself in the manner that Soupault had done three years earlier with respect to the earlier form of automatism employed in the composition of *The Magnetic Fields*.

The first formal attempts at psychic automatism took place at nine o'clock in the evening on 25 September 1922 at Breton's flat in the Rue Fontaine. The idea would seem to have originated from René Crevel, who had recently attended a spiritualist seance, and who claimed to be able to enter a trance state during which he could formulate reasonably coherent messages which were entirely unmediated by his consciousness. Although the spiritualist interpretation was universally rejected, it was decided that the Surrealists would try out the experiment for themselves. Simone Breton captures something of the atmosphere of these early seances in a letter written to her cousin, Denise: "Amazing things are happening here. [...] Spiritualism is not the word for it. A number of André's friends have discovered themselves to be incredibly gifted (that goes without saying) mediums. [...] It is dark. We are all sitting around the table in silence holding hands. Three minutes later at most and Crevel is already uttering hoarse groans and incomprehensible exclamations. Then in a determined, declamatory tone he launches into an atrocious story. A woman has drowned her husband, but it is he who asked her to do so. [...] There is a ferocity in every detail. Some obscenity too. [...] The most terrifying passages in *Maldoror* alone can give you any idea."[7]

Although initially sceptical (together with Breton he had recently unmasked two fraudulent hypnotists), it was Desnos who proved the most gifted medium. When the experiments were renewed (the participants now provided with paper and pencil), Desnos proved capable of furnishing incredible sequences of complicated puns, relating stories, and, as in the following example, replying to questions:

Q. — What do you know about Péret?
A. — He will die in a railway-carriage full of people.
Q. — Does that mean he will be assassinated?
A. — Yes.
Q. — By whom?
A. — [*He draws a train with a man falling out of the carriage window.*] By an animal.
Q. — What sort of animal?
A. — A blue ribbon, my sweet vagabond.[8]

Desnos excelled in the production of strange plays on words. Marcel Duchamp, in New York, had sent six such examples of these to *Littérature* where they had been published under the pseudonym Rrose Sélavy. On 7 October, in the course of one of the seances, Francis Picabia asked Desnos to produce something similar. He replied immediately, giving the first of a sequence of 138 such formulas which were published as a block the following month: *"Dans un temple en stuc de pomme le pasteur distillait le suc des psaumes."*9 As with most plays on words, this is largely untranslatable, though an approximate English version might read something like: "In a temple of apple plaster, the pastor distilled psalm cider." According to Breton in his essay on them in the same issue of *Littérature*, Desnos, like Duchamp, was only capable of producing these formulas when in a state of trance. Not only that, but Desnos also claimed to be reading Duchamp's mind in such a way that Rrose Sélavy would only speak to him when Duchamp had his eyes open.10

This is how Breton put the matter a few years later in *Nadja*:

I can still see Robert Desnos as he was in the days which those among us who have known them call the period of sleeping-fits. Then he would sleep, but he would also write, he would also speak. It is on some evening in my studio above the Cabaret du Ciel. "Come on in, come and see the Chat Noir," someone is shouting outside. And Desnos goes on seeing what I do not see, what I see only as he gradually reveals it to me. He borrows the personality of the most singular man alive, as well as the most deceptive and elusive — Marcel Duchamp. He has never seen him in the flesh. What in Duchamp seemed most inimitable in a few mysterious plays on words recurs in Desnos absolutely pure and suddenly takes on extraordinary resonance.

With respect to Rrose Sélavy's mysterious verbal puzzles Breton emphasised two distinctive characteristics in his original article: "firstly, their mathematical rigour (displacement of a letter towards a medial position in a word, exchange of a syllable between two words, etc.); secondly, the absence of the comical element which is usually considered to be inherent to the genre and which is the reason for its deprecation." If one regards the kind of increasingly sophisticated linguistic games which, in a somewhat different context, writers from Julien Torma (who it should not be forgotten corresponded with Desnos) to Unica Zürn (in her remarkable anagram poems) and Georges Perec of the Oulipo have engaged in as a continuation of these early experiments, then Breton was perhaps not entirely mistaken in his initial estimation of the apparently unlimited poetic possibilities they seemed to offer. *Liberty or Love!* contains numerous such verbal puzzles, puzzles which are by no means gratuitous. Corsair Sanglot's visit to the Sperm Drinkers' Club, for example, is entitled: À *la molle Berthe* (literally, "To flabby Berthe's"). *La molle Berthe*, however, is obviously also *la belle morte* ("lovely death"). One should never forget that, for Desnos, Rrose Sélavy is above all a reformulation of *Éros c'est la vie* ("Eros is life itself").

There is no doubt a certain element of deliberate mystification contained in some of Breton's accounts of these sessions. The Surrealists were by no means the only group to be interested in psychic phenomena at the time, and reference to some of the more exotic beliefs — such as thought transmission — connected with such practices might stimulate additional interest. However, the intentions behind these experiments into automatic writing were entirely serious. Dada's rejection of literature and its general anti-art provocations had led to a nihilistic and repetitive impasse. Breton and Paul Éluard especially were seeking a way out of this without returning to "literature" and "self-expression". Automatism seemed to offer this. Thus, the sessions of psychic automatism continued to be held on an almost daily basis during the last week of September and the first two weeks of October. They did not come to an end even when Breton and Picabia left for Barcelona in November. On the contrary, by the end of the year, they would seem — in Aragon's words — to have started to take on the proportions of an epidemic:

There were some seven or eight of us who now lived only for those moments of oblivion when, with the lights turned out, they spoke without consciousness, like men drowning in the open air. Every day they wanted to sleep more. They became intoxicated on their words when they were repeated back to them. They went into trances everywhere. All that was necessary now was to follow the opening ritual. In a café, amid all the voices, the bright lights and the bustle, Robert Desnos need only close his eyes, and he talks, and among the beers, the saucers, the whole ocean collapses with its prophetic racket, its vapours decorated with long oriflammes. However little he is encouraged by those who interrogate him, prophecy, the tone of magic, of revelation, of the French Revolution, the tone of the fanatic and the apostle, immediately follow. Under other conditions, Desnos, were he to maintain this delirium, would become the leader of a religion, the founder of a city, the tribune of a people in revolt.[11]

The seances were starting to get out of control, however, not only in terms of frequency but also with respect to the dangerous course they began to assume. On one occasion, at the home of a friend of Picabia, Crevel is said to have almost managed to persuade those under hypnosis to hang themselves from a set of coat pegs in a darkened room. On another occasion Breton had physically to restrain Desnos who, armed with a kitchen knife, had chased Éluard into the garden. Part of the problem perhaps stemmed from the temperament of the participants. Crevel, for example, has written about the rivalry which established itself between himself and Desnos — a rivalry which he believed might have pushed Desnos to physically attacking him, and which once led Crevel to bang Desnos's head against a mantelpiece. Eventually, Crevel claimed, he decided to have an operation for appendicitis in order to leave the field clear for Desnos in the hope that he would "get more strongly addicted and so go mad."[12] Breton, not unreasonably, finally felt compelled to call a halt to proceedings.

Liberty or Love!, though primarily a product of the kind of psychic automatism discussed above (Desnos dedicated at least one copy with an inscription to the effect that it was a novel written with his eyes closed), has not always been seen by commentators as a pure product of psychic automatism. Thus, the 'novel' — unlike Desnos's earlier *Mourning for Mourning* — has a certain number of characters, characters who would seem to show signs of having been partially determined in advance, characters who constantly encounter or just miss encountering each other in the course of their eternal wanderings. Indeed, the novel's protagonist, Corsair Sanglot, has been likened to — amongst others — Don Juan, Jack the Ripper, Fantômas, Captain Nemo, Nicholas Flamel and Maldoror. The work, moreover, has a greater thematic unity than might be expected of a purely automatic text and the action, or so it has been hinted, would in some sense seem to have been directed (the best evidence for this being the numerous self-referential passages).

However, if one examines the text more closely, a number of these objections — if objections they are — tend to evaporate. Take, for example, the names of Corsair Sanglot and Louise Lame. The hand of Rrose Sélavy would seem to be clearly at work here for three poetic pairings stand out: *Corsair/lame* [Corsair/wave], evocative of the sea; the sadistically erotic *Sanglot/larme* [Sob/tear]; and the idea of revolutionary violence contained in *sang/lame* [blood/blade]. Like the principal "characters", these three leitmotifs — the sea, eroticism and revolution — separate and converge into unexpected patterns throughout the novel. It is in these emerging patterns — perfect Surrealist combinations symbolising unconscious and conscious liberation initiated by love — that we must search for the elusive significance of the novel's title.

One of the most recurrent themes throughout all Desnos's writing is that of the sea and, more particularly, shipwreck. "I played on my own," he noted in his childhood reminiscences, *Confession d'un Enfant du siècle* (published in *La Révolution surréaliste* in 1926). "At six I lived in a dream world. My imagination nourished with maritime catastrophes, I travelled on beautiful sailing ships towards enchanted countries. The parquet tiles were easily mistaken for tumultuous waves, in my mind the armchair was a continent and the upright chairs deserted islands. Dangerous crossings. Sometimes *The Vengeance* would sink beneath my feet, at other times *The Medusa* would go down in a sea of freshly polished oak. I would have to swim towards the beach formed by the carpet. It was in this way that one day I became sexually aroused for the first time. I instinctively identified the feeling with the pangs of death and from that moment I contrived to die in the course of every crossing, drowning myself in featureless seas to the accompaniment of some lines of poetry I had come across by accident in a book I had been secretly reading [...] mixed in with a sense of voluptuous exhaustion." This childhood obsession is well in evidence in *Liberty or Love!* where the sea is both the kingdom of death and an enchanted arena which conceals untold marvels. Similarly, the idea of shipwreck serves as an extended metaphor for all the fears and anxieties connected with *l'amour passionnelle*.

This sense of transgression is strongly pronounced on both the erotic and the political levels in the novel's title. *La liberté ou la mort!* — a familiar cry in the streets of Paris after 1789 — is metamorphosed by Desnos into *la liberté ou l'amour!* The transmutation is an appropriate one given that the novel will suggest or describe, amongst much else, acts of fellatio, male homosexuality, sadism and tribadism. It is by acts such as these, however, that Corsair Sanglot and Louise Lame not so much affirm as demonstrate their refusal to be bound by the normal laws affecting the world. Just as night and the sea represent the possibility of unrestricted physical adventure, the body is the source of endless mental pleasure. Indeed, nothing — not even death — may impede the progress of those who are imbued with the sense of freedom conferred by the erotic.

That Desnos's poetic investigation of such ideas was in advance of the general tendency of Surrealism goes almost without saying, though the question of man's erotic nature would soon become the movement's central concern. Indeed, even as Desnos's novel remained stuck in legal limbo, the first seven of the twelve sessions of the *Recherches sur la sexualité* — published in English as *Investigating Sex. Surrealist Research, 1928-1932* — were taking place. "This word, love, upon which buffoons have strained their coarse wits to inflict every possible generalisation and corruption (filial love, divine love, love of the fatherland)," wrote Breton in 1929, "we are here, needless to say, restoring to its strict and threatening sense of total attachment to another human being."[13]

Breton's remarks prefaced the publication of the written response he had received to four questions concerning the nature of human sexuality. Three of those questions are of particular relevance to *Liberty or Love!* — (a) "What kind of hope do you place in love?"; (b) "How do you envisage the passage from the *idea* of love to the *fact* of loving? Willingly or not, would you sacrifice your freedom for love? Have you ever done so?"; (c) "Do you believe in the victory of love's glory over the sordidness of life, or in the victory of the sordidness of life over love's glory?"

In her Afterword to *Investigating Sex*, Dawn Ades claims that although the conversations of the Surrealists on the nature of human sexuality "were, are still, astounding, unprecedented and unmatched in their frankness and intimacy," they were regarded as something of a failure at the time. Breton would certainly seem to have hoped for a greater degree of unanimity in the responses. In an essay on the erotic written in 1923 but unpublished until 1953, Desnos had already concluded that "the erotic is an individual science": "Everyone resolves as far as they can the secondary questions, but they are in accord with their fellows only to the extent of noting the insolubility of the eternal questions, the existence of which we never tire of proclaiming."[14] Not surprisingly, Desnos's reply to Breton's questions — printed in the same issue of *La Révolution surréaliste* as the latter's pronouncement of his "excommunication" — was short-tempered to say the least.

Elsewhere in the same essay Desnos remarks: "Any philosophy whose morality does not contain an 'EROTIC' is incomplete. [...] Equally, what man, preoccupied with the infinite in time and space, has not constructed this 'EROTIC' in the secret of his soul; what man caring about poetry, disturbed by contingent or remote mysteries, does not like to withdraw into that spiritual retreat in which love is at once absolutely pure and licentious?" This seeming paradox between a love which is at once pure and licentious finds a corollary in *Liberty or Love!* in the narrator's quest for the unique woman (Chapter II contains an echo of Breton's remark in *Les Pas perdus* as to how he would leave his bedroom door open at night in the hope of a visit from a mysterious unknown woman), a quest some critics have found strangely at odds with Corsair Sanglot's libertine conduct. A number of ingenious solutions have been proposed in the attempt to resolve this conflict. The conflict only exists, however, when one attempts to impose the conventional moralistic — and therefore false — standards of psychological realism on the novel. Indeed, it might be said that this is precisely the reconciliation — even dialectical! — that the title of the novel promises.

What hope did Desnos place in love? For Desnos, eroticism was not only the guarantee of personal freedom, it was also the guarantee of political freedom. Eroticism, he implies, would prove to be the catalyst for the radical change in the social structure by which love could be freed from necessity. Given the social regime in France, supported by the still powerful Catholic Church, which viewed procreation within the family as a patriotic duty, the humoristic profanation of Catholic doctrine which runs through the novel should be seen as integral to the work. Desnos's radicalism, already noted by Aragon, was also observed by Breton ("Desnos is more revolutionary than the Revolution," he once remarked) and Leiris (in whom Desnos confided that his first names, Robert Pierre, almost constituted Robespierre).[15]

This radicalism finds its most sustained expression in the numerous descriptions concerning the advent of the new religion — which proves to be largely a parody of the old one — presided over by Bébé Cadum (see overleaf). Like the three enamel painters, who also take on a mystical significance, Bébé Cadum was, in fact, well known to Parisians at the time. Indeed, they saw him every day, staring down at them from the advertising hoardings, for Cadum was a brand of soap being widely publicised at the time by means of the head of a monstrous, smiling baby. If this mythologising of an advertising hoarding seems innocent enough, some of the other religious symbolism in the book was taken to task by the courts. Almost the whole of Chapter VII was censored, together with the first two pages of Chapter VIII and a long passage in Chapter IX. These three passages deal with such matters as the Sperm Drinkers' Club and a parody of the Eucharist in which the bread and the wine are replaced by some sort of soap-covered sponge which succeeds in celebrating both female contraception (a traditional use of sponge) and the elixir of the new god (Bébé Cadum's sperm).

Unrestricted by the claims of time and space, the novel is able to telescope the crucifixion of Christ, the execution of Louis XVI in 1793 and the multiple deaths, presented as contemporaneous with the writing of the novel, of Corsair Sanglot. This leads to some extraordinary juxtapositions: "Christ is finally worthy of his name: he is crucified upon a cross of oak decorated with tricolour pennants resembling a platform on 14 July. At its foot, a dozen or so musicians are playing catchy tunes on brass instruments." (p.57 below) Christ, it is implied, was responsible for bringing repression into the world. By bringing forward the crucifixion to 1793, Desnos is able to depict the joyful celebrations which mark the end of both political and religious tyranny. Inversely, though equally blasphemously, the Marquis de Sade, who is perceived as the architect of that freedom (especially in the sexual domain), later in the novel is in turn deified by the portrayal of his sufferings in order to save mankind…

Such elements are essential to a novel which seeks to desacralise bourgeois conceptions of love. Needless to say, as in the current French edition, the various passages which were mutilated or censored by the Tribunal Correctionnel de la Seine have been restored in the present edition.

Bébé Cadum and Bibendum Michelin (cf. Chapter III and note to p.54)

One problem which has continued to vex critics is the question why the author chose to preface his novel with a poem attributed to Rimbaud but which was, in fact, composed by Desnos himself. There are, I think, a number of related reasons mitigating in favour of the inclusion of this strange, albeit powerful, homage to Rimbaud — reasons it is perhaps worthwhile briefly outlining here.

If one forgets for a moment the spurious attribution, there are innumerable thematic links between "The Night-Watch" and *Liberty or Love!* Both are voyages, voyages which are governed not by geographical, chronological or physical laws, voyages in which the reader is free to participate as he or she feels fit, voyages which the author may bring to an abrupt conclusion at any moment. Both are adventure stories, adventure stories which may take place on the seabed (evoked in stanza 40 of the poem, for example, and again in relation to Corsair Sanglot's underwater exploits in Chapter IV); on the streets of Paris (that privileged Surrealist arena for erotic encounter); during the Revolution (whether of 1789, 1848 or 1871). Both, while permeated with primitive Christian symbolism (the mysterious reference to the "boned hysteria" stabbing "stigmata in our palms" of stanza 4, for example, is later explained (p.53) in passing by reference to the fact that fish have long been dedicated to the "cult of divine objects"), may obviously be perceived in a sense as "blasphemous" (e.g. the birth of Christ evoked in the seventh stanza which points directly towards the author's later remark about strangling the child in the second chapter). Examples of this kind may be multiplied at will. More than this, however, the final stanza of the poem announces the main purpose of the novel. *Liberty or Love!* will be nothing less than an investigation of the relationship which exists between the two ideas of the title.

Another explanation which suggests itself for the inclusion of the pseudo-Rimbaud's "The Night-Watch" is that the poem represents an attempt on behalf of the author to wrestle Rimbaud away from the grasp of those Catholic writers who were laying siege to his literary reputation at the time. Rimbaud's work and the legend of his life — his rebellions, his renunciation of poetry, his self-imposed exile in Africa — exercised a strong fascination over the Dadaists and Surrealists. Indeed, it is difficult to overemphasise the importance of Rimbaud in the creation of the Surrealist consciousness. In his *Entretiens* (1952), Breton recounts how he wandered the streets of Nantes in 1916 totally possessed by the spirit of Rimbaud. Later, in the *First Manifesto of Surrealism*, he proclaims: "Rimbaud is Surrealist in the way he lived, and elsewhere."

In Rimbaud, both in his rejection of traditional aesthetic values and in the non-conformity of his life, the Dadaists believed they saw a kindred figure who glorified rupture and negation. Elevated to the same rank as Lautréamont by the Surrealists, Rimbaud was the poet-alchemist, a visionary maker of images who, by deranging the senses in order to uncover the unconscious sources of the poetic imagination, paved the way for automatic writing. This is a point implicitly made by Aragon in *Une Vague de rêves* (1924) when he says that one result of those early experiments into automatic writing was the sense of "an incomparable freedom, a liberation of the mind, an unprecedented production of images." Suddenly, the great poetic unity that emanates from "the prophetic books of all peoples to *Les Illuminations* and *Les Chants de Maldoror*" became accessible: "*Une saison en Enfer* shed its riddles."

The Surrealists, however, were not alone in claiming Rimbaud as one of their own. There was also a Christian interpretation which was gaining converts. This was a trend which began soon after the poet's death in 1891 when his sister put forward the somewhat unlikely claim that he had "died like a saint" after leading a life of virtue. This was a theme which Paul Claudel, himself a recent convert to Catholicism, developed in an important article published in 1912 and reprinted four years later in the form of a preface to an edition of Rimbaud's works. During the Twenties and Thirties. This view of a Catholic Rimbaud was articulated with ever greater conviction. Indeed, in 1930, Kra — the publisher of *Liberty or Love!* — brought out an edition of two essays by the critic Jacques Rivière, written more than fifteen years previously, which his widow, an intransigent Catholic, had somehow managed to amend so as to include remarks to the effect that Rimbaud, if not actually a practising Christian, "nevertheless provides a marvellous introduction to Christianity."[16]

Naturally, this gave rise to a lively — on occasion, acrimonious — debate during these two decades. In August 1924, for example, Aragon and Breton signed, not without a certain relish, a short preface to a previously unpublished text by Rimbaud which considerably undermined the legend of a Catholic Rimbaud. Claudel — mainly as a result of an article in which he had described the Surrealists' activities as "pederastic" — was the target of personal attack the following year: "We consider Rimbaud to be a man who had lost hope in his salvation and whose work and life bear unequivocal testimony to his damnation." Finally, in 1927, the year *Liberty or Love!* was published, the Surrealist group brought out a highly polemical tract mocking the pretensions of the inhabitants of Charleville in the Ardennes who wished to erect a statue commemorating Rimbaud's birth.[17] Desnos was amongst the signatories. Nothing would seem more plausible than that the latter intended "The Night-Watch" to add more fuel to the controversy.

Finally, the inclusion of a poem written in alexandrine verse with a spurious attribution to Rimbaud was perhaps intended as a double act of defiance towards Breton. If this was so, Desnos selected his weapons skilfully. Firstly, because the purely literary constraints of the alexandrine verse form — even if employed by Rimbaud in "*Le Bateau ivre*" — were exactly the opposite of the liberating effects Breton sought to achieve through automatism. Indeed, Desnos would seem to have gone out of his way to taunt Breton on the subject for, according to the latter in the *Second Manifesto*, he managed to have inserted in a newspaper a report about him serenading Breton with alexandrine verses of his composition on a beach in Cuba. It would be an understatement to say that Breton was not amused. Secondly, Breton was extremely sensitive — as he demonstrated more than twenty years later over the publication of a spurious poem by Rimbaud entitled "*La Chasse spirituelle*" — to the issue of the false attributions of texts to Rimbaud. "I do not believe that this poem ["The Night-Watch"] adds one whit to Desnos's glory," wrote Breton — who otherwise admired the novel which accompanied it — in 1930.

By then it hardly mattered. Relations between Desnos and various members of the Surrealist movement had been strained for some time. Indeed, it has been claimed that he never forgave Breton for calling a halt to the experiments in psychic automatism a few years earlier. Breton pronounced the sentence in the *Second Manifesto*; Desnos replied in the pages of the collective pamphlet *Un Cadavre* and by issuing his own *Third Manifesto of Surrealism* in which he demanded that it was time Surrealism entered the public domain.

"The only word that still excites me is liberty," wrote Breton in the *First Manifesto*. For the adventurous hero of *Liberty or Love!*, the notion of friendship, like that of love, is a trap — one to be avoided at any cost. Neither can exist except where there is total autonomy of action. "I know the feeling of being abandoned only too well," writes Desnos in the course of the novel, "having experienced it myself. If that is the insolent luxury you desire, that is fine; you may follow me. Otherwise all I ask of you is your indifference, if not your enmity."

Like Corsair Sanglot, Desnos did not merely affirm such principles, he lived them — not only in the rarefied atmosphere of the French avant-garde, but also in the more dangerous world that was to come. Although it is beyond the bounds of this introduction to consider his later work, written in the 1930s and early 1940s, long after he had broken with the Surrealist movement (he became increasingly involved in the "public domain" — especially cinema and the radio), it is important to note that by the time his last novel was published in 1942, Desnos had already been an active member of the French Resistance for two years. When the Gestapo came to arrest him in February 1944, he was in the middle of preparing a satirical underground journal. Sent first to Fresnes, then on to Compiègne, he was finally deported to Buchenwald at the end of April. Germany was already on the brink of collapse. The inmates were forced to begin a long and exhausting exodus towards Terezine (Theresienstadt) in Czechoslovakia. It was there that Robert Desnos died of typhus in June 1945, a few days after his liberation.

NOTES

1. *"Robert Desnos"*, *Le Journal littéraire*, 5 July 1924.

2. André Breton, *Manifestes du surréalisme*, Gallimard, 1979, p.42.

3. Desnos's account of this meeting is to be found in *Nouvelles Hébrides et autres textes, 1922-1930*, (ed.) Marie-Claire Dumas, Gallimard, 1978, pp.302-5.

4. André Breton, *Entrée des médiums*, now in *Les Pas perdus*, Gallimard, 1974, p.124.

5. *Manifestes du surréalisme, op. cit.*, p.32.

6. *Entrée des médiums, op. cit.*, pp.123-4.

7. Cited by Marguerite Bonnet in *André Breton, Naissance de l'aventure surréaliste*, Corti, 1975, pp.263-4.

8. First published in *Littérature (nouvelle série)*, No. 6, 1 Nov. 1922, pp.8-12.

9. *"Rrose Sélavy"*, *Littérature (n.s.)*, No. 7, 1 Dec. 1922, pp.14-22.

10. *"Les mots sans rides"*, now in *Les Pas perdus*, pp.138-41.

11. Louis Aragon, *"Une Vague de rêves"*, *Commerce*, No. 2, 1924, pp.105-6.

12. René Crevel, *"The Period of Sleeping-Fits"*, *This Quarter*, No. 5, 1932, p.186.

13. *Investigating Sex. Surrealist Research, 1928-1932* (ed. José Pierre; tr. Malcolm Imrie), Verso, p.157.

14. *De l'érotisme considéré dans ces manifestations écrites et du point de vue de l'esprit moderne*, now in *Nouvelles Hébrides*, p.110.

15. André Breton, *"Robert Desnos"*, *op. cit.*, p.474; Michel Leiris, *"Robert Desnos, 'Une Parole d'or'"*, *Cahiers l'Herne*, No. 54, 1987, p.368. Desnos's psychic preoccupation with the French Revolution is quite manifest in one of the seances (that of 30 Sept. 1922): "They will become whiter than the hated pennant of the monarchy... Cowards, cowards... And this white collar for which you reproach me as an unneccessary adornment... You are jealous of the elegant neck which comes out of it... You are blacksmiths escaped from your nocturnal forges... nocturnal... The guillotine... The guillotine... I am alone. You are the multitude and you quake before my severe regard." Elsewhere, Breton refers to Desnos as one of the most *frénétique* figures — a term usually applied to such marginalised figures of the French Romantic movement as Pétrus Borel and Charles Lassailly — of the Surrealist movement. (*"Sur Robert Desnos"*, *Cahiers l'Herne*, p.346)

16. Jacques Rivière, *Rimbaud*, Kra, 1930, p.232.

17. Aragon and Breton's preface to Rimbaud's *Un Cœur sous une soutane*, together with the collective tracts entitled *Lettre ouverte à M. Paul Claudel* and *Permettez!* may all be found in: *Tracts surréalistes et déclarations collectives, 1922-1939*, (ed.) José Pierre, Vol. 1, Le Terrain vague, 1980.

LIBERTY OR LOVE!

To the Revolution.
To Love
To she who is their incarnation.[1]

The Night-Watch

by Arthur Rimbaud

Above the vague yet hard-edged coastline may
Those lighthouses that scan the foaming tide
Shine over masts in peril night and day
Doomed innocently to be crucified.

May frail horizon's tight-rope hear the cry
Columbus turned into an S.O.S.
Before his prancing prayers were answered by
The sands where Friday's footprints softly press.

And may — proud pilot of the vasty deep
Whose wake wipes out, as golden sunshine dawns,
All civil infamy that wise men keep —
A negro monarch turn us back to fauns.

We've swallowed shoals of fish and felt their boned
Hysteria stab stigmata in our palms
Inducing dreamy mystic meetings; groaned
When swollen stomachs gave our journey qualms.

We'll sleep for many nights, heads wreathed in leaves
As pillows, all brutalities forget
Until some gently frowning dream deceives
Us into seeking one more city yet.

The star that saved lost sailors — old sea-dogs
Whose great moustaches snatched at tempests, tossed
Into their twirls when planets burst through fogs —
Could not restore the vigour we had lost.

How good that one Wise Man, when time drew near,
Scrabbling amongst the swaddling-clothes and straw,
Proclaimed divine births, trembling out of fear,
And sad fists pressed our eyeballs red and raw.

It's all too much! Walls and squares must be succumbed!
And crumble! Star-trekked to the rocky main
Those creaking sails creaked, replete with bleeding-gummed
Conquerors of the unrequited slain.

For us, however, with our guts so far
Unstung by hemlock, free from nettle's toll,
In narrow-hearted towns — this carfax star
Sways into twilight with a hammock's roll.

A light switched on, as shuffling footsteps pass,
Silhouettes one firm breast in beams;
A voice more frequent than sharp shards of glass
Smashes to smithereens our packaged dreams.

While cross-roads shook with rifle-shots' intrigue,
Recalling feats and banquets long ago,
The constables-in-chief sensed their fatigue
And sadly nodded where high attics glow.

Once we played hopscotch in bold grids of light
Blinking — and then abandoning our games
When coachmen's gates clanged hard or, late at night,
Cabs passed us occupied by blowsy dames.

Despairing when our fingers let love slip
Through them — a grass snake off to pastures new
Without a thought for how we might equip
Our fates, sad beadles weeping in a pew,

Distraught, inadequate in terms of sex —
We'd swig, to be convinced of comfort's lies
Emerald potions' potent bubbling flecks,
Till mammal-based Nirvana cleared our eyes.

Once overcome, grief cast more healing spells
Than herbal cures or warm seductive drinks.
We all attained our own platonic hells,
Raw hearts slain, naked, by a tiger-sphinx.

Our teeth of stainless steel beat scurvy's screams
And bit doubloons to spit out golden pips,
But, weak from aimless echelons of dreams,
Blood brought back colour to our twisted lips.

Pneumatic females glimpsed across a room
Whilst folding cami-knickers, pink and white,
Our kisses taught your nascent breasts to bloom
When stallioned relief arrived by night!

Cry-babies, quiet! Memories are born
In strict progression like warm circling dunes;
We've led cud-chewing cowards by the horn,
Of destiny's false fortune's piper's tunes.

Leave us alone — we choking, short-breathed Don
Juans, numb-knuckled, muscles over-stressed
From putting up with rigid rules. We've gone
With blistered feet through one too many test.

Now dodging in between each street-lamp's pool
We beg the turquoise pavements of desire
To reinvigorate our tom-cat's cool
And sleepy hearts with adolescent fire.

Avenging railways, your pursuit is vain.
We'll live if needs be in a commune, blind
And deaf, and leave the fragrant herb-green lane
With black-backed randy splashing sharks behind.

Sprung from a sleepless heart's profound abyss
Recurrent nightmares wrack the dormant town.
What night of lobster-tentacles rips this
Raw eye? Which Etna flings its lava down?

More isolated in suburban waste
Than legionnaires lost in Saharan sand
A rattling drum-roll in our throats has chased
The grey-faced bourgeoisie beyond the land.

Our bloodshot pupils conjure up a dream
Of distant signal-men parading, fast
Asleep, dishevelled, lecherous, they seem
To lift their lids when an express zooms past.

At crossings herdsmen clench an angry fist
In futile protest at the wagon's roar.
Stay with your cattle and the wives you've kissed;
Obey the church's pointless semaphore.

Will no flames cause these ancient stones to flare
In twisted vaults with crippled nave and pew?
Will some restored and ruthless Robespierre
Render their cattle to the chosen few?

The sullen flame that flickers round the pyx
May spread to lick the puffy jowl that prays
Till festive fire-brigades with torchlit wicks
Extinguish three dead gods in one last blaze.

No point in *rigor mortis*, Christ, with slack
Limbs crucified — you've not seen dead fish crowned
With venom's thorn-distilling sea-green wrack
That staunches wine-dark wounds of men long drowned.

In cities where the gas-lamps serenade
The ballroom's chandeliers, strength is deployed
To latch lust's kisses on the leering maid —
Then wonderfully is your church destroyed.

With sudden menace, night-watch troops emerge
Erecting wooden compounds, then they cough
In breathless huddles, till fierce storms upsurge
To ward oppressive sleep and boredom off.

They warm numb fingers round a brazier's glow
And see romantic ruins crumble, then
As chills run up their spines, they long to know
If heroes in the *Odyssey* beat ten

Thousand fierce rats or more; then, where in shreds
A poster on a bare wall flaps and sags,
They picture lovers with their close-locked heads
And pick their own loves over like old rags

That daybreak beggars go through after nights
Of silken loot, like frankincense and myrrh
Or gold, then daydream — if a snowstorm bites
Into their card-white cheeks — of boots of fur.

Black nostrils stuffed with filthy snuff, they yawn
Huddled over bakers' grilles where fresh-baked bread
Shoots soft warm air to fight the frosty dawn
Whilst sprawling hangmen wake in their own bed.

When their assistants in town squares erect,
Scaffolds, perspiring, cursing, out of breath,
Our searching eyes and groping fists select
Breasts to swell thoughts of love or, if not, death.

Huddled around dead embers they observe
Swift milkmen darting through the narrow streets
As, mixed with mist, long morning shadows swerve
And coppers round up stray tarts from their beats.

We don't invigilate romantic bliss
For midnight ghouls stain hollow sockets black;
Our mouths dripped blood beneath their satin kiss,
As startled cheeks blushed when the blood ran back.

We sit in expectation at the base
Of gibbets till some new Apocalypse
Unbinds love's cords that torture and enlace
Us, though banned names like ours soil no one's lips.

As boys at play lance catapults at spines
Of jewelled ladies married off to earls,
Fierce Prosperos, we shipwreck merchant lines
And eat the corpses, we whose love for girls

Was killed by cholera, we saints that cast
Our nets on oyster-banks in bloody seas,
Slice ropes that hold and anchor steam-boats fast
Or plaits that schoolgirls swing with lazy ease.

We hate these watch-nights when obscene regrets
Devour the old, when spiders that eat fowl
Increase their yard-armed lusts, square-rigged like nets,
And scabies throbs aflamed with horrid howl.

On flagships' bridges, ensigns watch squids prey
On lobsters in submerged wrecked hulks; then fight
While drooping signals drip; in comfort they
Sank through the concave sea one party night.

The band played waltzes; dancers tailed in black
Found partners they had never seen before;
Love weighted down with gold sank in a sack;
On rafts nude millionaires' wives left the shore.

Through tarnished glass the café's counter shines
Where puppet-wires suspend humanity;
Things past and things to come, things man declines
Decline in facet-worded Trinity.

At times we catch our fingers unawares
On steamed-up windows doodling leaves and plants;
While on the river tough tugs chug their wares
To port, and bridges dress up for a dance.

Too scared to drown our sorrows with a bare
Self-slaughtered bodkin 'gainst this sea of pigs,
With slapped-on lipstick, our mascara'd stare
Winks, nods at passion's mimicked periwigs.

Our wrists are handcuffed by the eyes of girls.
And why do faces fascinate our quests?
Why should we wait? The fritter's song unfurls.
Our eyes will bleed from rose-thorns in girls' breasts.

Why should we watch by night? Long, long ago,
Jesus performed a miracle each year
At Christmas. On that crisp and even snow
Emmanuel's unsmirched feet felt no cold fear.

Our feet are sucked down in thick traitrous slime
Which swallowed Christ's cadavers, white as bleach,
Engulfed July's wise prayers; popes — all the same time
In mitres — flew, then sank beyond all reach.

Since then we watch and scrutinise dark night
In expectation that bright dawn will see
A girl swim through the breaking waves of light
Till love be reconciled with liberty.

26 November - 1 December 1923

I. *Robert Desnos*

Born in Paris, 4 July 1900.
Died in Paris, 13 December 1924, the day on which he wrote these lines.

II. *The Depths of Night*

When I reached the street, the leaves were falling from the trees. The staircase behind me was no more than a firmament sprinkled with stars among which I could clearly distinguish the footsteps of a certain woman whose Louis XV heels had for a long time drummed the macadam of the paths where sand lizards scurried, timid creatures tamed by me, then invited into my lodgings where they made common cause with my sleep. The Louis XV heels pursued them. I can assure you that this period of my life, when each nocturnal minute marked the carpet of my room with a new imprint, was a most remarkable one: a strange mark which sometimes made me shiver. How many times, in stormy weather or by the light of the moon, did I get up to contemplate by the gleam of a log fire, or that of a match, or a glow-worm, those memories of women who had come to my bed, completely naked apart from stockings and high-heeled slippers retained out of respect for my desire, and more unaccountable than a parasol found floating in the middle of the Pacific by a steamship. Marvellous heels against which I scratched my feet! On which road do you ring now and shall I see you ever again? My door was always open to mystery then, but mystery came in, closing it behind her, and ever since I have heard, without a word being spoken, an immense trampling of feet, that of the crowd of naked women laying siege to my keyhole. The profusion of their Louis XV heels makes a sound comparable to that of logs burning in the hearth, to fields of ripe corn, to clocks in deserted rooms at night, to a strange breathing on the same pillow next to your face.

Meanwhile, I turned into the Rue des Pyramides. The wind wafted leaves torn from the trees in the Tuileries, leaves which fell to the ground with a soft sound. They were gloves; gloves of every description, kid gloves, suede gloves, long Lisle gloves. A woman is taking off her gloves in front of a jeweller's to try on a ring and have her hand kissed by Corsair Sanglot, a chanteuse stands at the back of the stage of a rowdy theatre awash with the effluvia of the guillotine and cries of "Revolution", a tiny bit of hand shows through where the buttons fasten. From time to time, heavier than a meteorite at its journey's end, a boxer's glove falls. The crowd trampled these memories of kisses and embraces underfoot without paying them the deference they deserved. I alone avoided treading on them. Sometimes I even picked one up. It thanked me with a warm embrace. I felt it tremble in my trouser pocket. Its mistress must have trembled just like that in a fleeting moment of love. I walked on.

Retracing my steps and going along under the arcades of the Rue de Rivoli, I finally saw Louise Lame walking ahead of me.

The wind buffeted the city. The hoardings of Bébé Cadum beckoned the emissaries of the storm to them and under those watchful eyes the entire city writhed in convulsions.

There were at first two gloves, clutching each other in an invisible handshake, their shadow dancing for a long time before me.

Before me? No, it was Louise Lame, walking in the direction of the Étoile. Singular promenade! In bygone times, kings walked in the direction of a star which was neither more nor less concrete than you, Place de l'Étoile, with your arch, the orbit in which the sun lodges like the eye of the sky, adventurous promenade whose mysterious objective is perhaps you whom I solicit, fatal, exclusive and murderous love. If I had been one of the kings, you would have been strangled in your cradle, O Jesus, for having interrupted my glorious voyage so soon, and for having destroyed my liberty since a mystic love doubtless would have fettered me and dragged me like a prisoner along all the high-roads of the globe which I had dreamed of travelling as a free man.

I took pleasure in watching the play of her fur coat against her neck, of the swish of the hem against her silk stockings, of the imagined rubbing of the silk lining against her hips. Suddenly, I noticed the presence of a white border around her calves. This border grew rapidly, slipped to the ground, and when I reached the spot where it had fallen I picked up a pair of exquisite cambric cami-knickers. They fitted perfectly in my hand. I unfolded them and plunged my head into them with delight. They were impregnated with Louise Lame's most intimate odours. What fabulous whale, of whatever colour, could distil a more fragrant ambergris. Fishermen, lost in the fragments of the ice floes, who permit yourselves to perish from an emotion strong enough to cause you to fall into the icy waves when, once the monster has been hacked to pieces, the blubber and the oil and the whale bones necessary for the manufacture of corsets and umbrellas carefully garnered, you discover the cylinder of precious matter in the yawning belly. Louise Lame's cami-knickers! What a universe! By the time I regained a sense of my surroundings, she had got a head start on me. Tripping over the gloves which were now embracing one another, my head swimming, I set out after her, guided by her leopard-skin coat.

At the Porte Maillot, I recovered the black silk dress where she had discarded it. Naked, now she was naked under the fur coat. The evening breeze was charged with the sharp odour of canvas sails picked up off the coast, charged with the odour of partly-dried seaweed washed up on the beach, charged with the smoke of locomotives en route for Paris, charged with the odour of hot rails after the passage of the fast express, charged with the fragile yet penetrating perfume of damp grassy lawns extending in front of sleeping *châteaux*, charged with the odour of the cement of churches under construction, the heavily laden evening breeze would be rushing in under her coat, caressing her hips and the underside of her breasts. The rubbing of the cloth against her hips must undoubtedly have begun to arouse her, even as she walked down the Allée des Acacias towards an unknown destination.

Cars crossed one another in the street, their headlights sweeping over the trees, the ground bristling with hummocks, Louise Lame hurried on. I could clearly distinguish the leopard-skin coat.

It must have been a ferocious animal.

For many years he had terrorised the surrounding countryside. From time to time, his supple form could be glimpsed silhouetted upon the lower branch of a tree or on a rock, then, the following dawn, caravans of giraffes and antelopes, on their way to watering-holes, bore witness among the natives to a bloody epic that had deeply etched its claws into the trunks of the forest. That went on for several years. The corpses, if corpses could speak, would have been able to say that his fangs were white and his powerful tail more dangerous than the cobra, but the dead cannot speak, still less skeletons, still less the skeletons of giraffes, for these gracious animals were the leopard's favourite prey.

One October day, as the sky turned green, the hills standing on the horizon saw the leopard, disdainful for once of the antelopes, mustangs and proud, gracious and nimble giraffes, crawl to a thicket of thorns. All night and all the following day he rolled on the ground and roared. By the rising of the moon, he had completely flayed himself, and his skin, intact, lay on the ground. The leopard had not stopped growing during all this time. As the moon came out, he reached the tops of the highest trees, by midnight his shadow unhooked the stars.

It was an extraordinary sight to watch the progress of this skinless leopard across the countryside where the darkness deepened with his gigantic shadow. He dragged his skin behind him, a skin such as no Roman emperor had ever worn the equal, neither they nor the most handsome legionnaire whom they loved.

Processions of flags and of lictors, processions of fire-flies, miraculous ascensions! Nothing was ever more surprising than the progress of this bleeding beast, its blue veins bulging.

When he reached the house of Louise Lame, the door opened of its own accord and the leopard had just sufficient energy before dying to deposit the supreme homage of his fur on the steps at the feet of the fatal, adorable girl.

His bones still obstruct a number of roads around the world. The echo of his howl of rage, after having reverberated for many years over glaciers and crossroads, is as dead as the sound of the tides and Louise Lame walks before me, naked under her coat.

A few more steps and then she unfastens this last item of clothing. It falls to the ground. I run faster. Louise Lame is now naked, completely naked in the Bois de Boulogne. The cars flee, trumpeting like elephants, their headlights illuminating now a birch tree, now Louise Lame's thigh without attaining, however, the pubic fleece. A storm of anguished sounds spreads through the surrounding districts: Puteaux, Saint-Cloud, Billancourt.

The naked woman continues on her way accompanied by the flap of invisible cloth; Paris bars its doors and windows, extinguishes its lamps. A murderer in a remote district struggles to kill an imperturbable pedestrian. Piles of bones obstruct the streets. The naked woman knocks on every door, lifts each closed eyelid.

From the top of a building, Bébé Cadum, magnificently illuminated, announces better times ahead. A man watches from his window. He is waiting. What is he waiting for?

The ringing of an alarm wakes a corridor. On the street, a door shuts.

A car goes by.

Bébé Cadum, magnificently illuminated, remains alone, attentive observer of the events which, let us hope, shall be staged in the street.

III. *Everything Visible is Made of Gold*

Corsair Sanglot dons his full attire, a familiar sight on the turbulent streets and macadam pavements. Life carries on just as it pleases in Paris or anywhere else in the world; an amiable voice directs him on his way. This leads him to the Tuileries where he meets Louise Lame. There are those coincidences which, although they do not stir up the countryside, are none the less of more significance than dikes and lighthouses, than peaceful frontiers and the calm of nature in unfrequented places at the moment explorers chance to pass. It is of little consequence to know what the preliminaries were to the conversation which took place between our hero and heroine. None but the strongest and most ferocious of the beasts of love could have held out against their fangs and claws. The guardians of the Tuileries merely saw a strange couple talking with animation and then going off together down the Rue du Mont-Thabor. A hotel bedroom offered them asylum. It was a poetic setting, in which a pitcher of water assumed the significance of a reef along some wild, romantic coastline; a dangling light-bulb was more sinister than three fir trees in the middle of an emerald green field on a Sunday afternoon; and a mirror brought to life menacing, autonomous individuals. Hotel bedroom furnishings unknown to the most outdated copywriters; furnishings evocative of crime itself! In the presence of such objects Jack the Ripper had executed one of his most splendid transgressions by way of which men are reminded from time to time that love is not merely just some kind of pleasantry. Magnificent furniture! The white water pitcher, the basin and the dressing-table silently recalling that red liquid which had once made them respectable. Journalists had published photographs of these modest props, elevating them to landscapes in the manner I have just suggested. They had been summoned to appear at the Assize Courts along with the evidence for the prosecution. Singular tribunal! Nobody had ever managed to arrest Jack the Ripper and the dock for the accused remained empty. The judges had been appointed from amongst the oldest blind men in Paris. The press gallery was overflowing with people. And at the rear, the general public, held back by a cordon of policemen, consisted of an assemblage of pot-bellied bourgeoisie. Over all these silent individuals there hovered a buzzing swarm of flies. The trial lasted eight days and eight nights and when, at its close, a miraculous verdict was returned against the unknown assassin, the water pitcher, the basin and the dressing-table with the little soap-dish on which a tiny bar of pinkish soap could still be found were all returned to that room which had been marked by the passage of an extraordinary being.

Louise Lame and Corsair Sanglot, who respected few things for their moral value, respectfully considered these remains of an adventure which could have been their own. Then, after staring each other out, they undressed. When they were naked, Corsair Sanglot stretched out across the bed, so that his feet still touched the floor, and Louise Lame knelt before him.

Magisterial kiss of enemy mouths.

Reproduction is proper to the species, but love is proper to the individual. I prostrate myself before you, low kisses of the flesh. I too have plunged my head into the shadowy recess of thighs. Louise Lame clasped her handsome lover tightly. Her eyes sought out the effect this conjunction of her tongue on his flesh had on his face. It is a mysterious rite, and perhaps the most beautiful. When Corsair Sanglot's breath turned into a pant, Louise Lame became more resplendent than the male.

The eyes of the latter wandered about the room. They came to rest eventually on a block calendar. It had been forgotten by a shifty book-keeper divided in his desire to forget time and to be able to measure it mechanically, without any thought as to the utter stupidity of such pretensions.

In any event, Corsair Sanglot knew very well the date on which the calendar had stopped. Every year he was drawn to read the same item of news which, though now half a century old, never failed to evoke the same feverishness within him. It was on such a day that he had first read the brittle strip of paper, and ever since he had had no choice but, fatally, to repeat the same action every year.

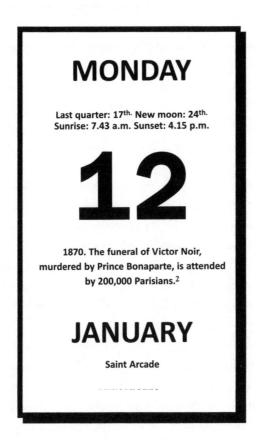

MONDAY

Last quarter: 17th. New moon: 24th.
Sunrise: 7.43 a.m. Sunset: 4.15 p.m.

12

1870. The funeral of Victor Noir,
murdered by Prince Bonaparte, is attended
by 200,000 Parisians.[2]

JANUARY

Saint Arcade

And the thoughts of Corsair Sanglot followed a trail into the heart of a virgin forest.

He arrived in a gold-mining town. A provocatively dressed Spanish woman was dancing in a dance-hall. He followed her into a garret room where the muted echoes of altercations and the orchestra could still be heard. He undressed her himself, removing each garment with a languor charged with wisdom and rich in emotion. The bed then became the scene of a savage fight, he bit her, she defended herself screaming, while the dancer's lover, a formidable half-caste, banged at the door.

It was a merciless siege. Revolver shots were fired through the oak partitions, splintering the mirrors where the silver was silently peeling as a result of the many long years they had spent reflecting fatal passions. Spurred on by his opponent's courage, the Spaniard fired through the window at the crowd of horsemen and vigilantes intent on a lynching. The lovers finally escaped over the roofs. Angry cries filled the town, lassos were hastily knotted, but, arriving at the inner courtyard, the pursuers spotted the absence of the twin black mares which were so fast that any hope of overtaking them was out of the question. Abandoning the fugitives to their fate, the men dispersed amongst the local bars.

Out of danger, and several miles from town, Corsair Sanglot and the Spanish woman came to a halt. Their love no longer existed, except as a dream. They went off in opposite directions. Forests through which a path must be hacked with machetes, draped with tropical creepers and enormous fallen trees, prairies, snow-covered steppes, battles against Indians, stolen sledges, slain deer, you haven't seen the invisible Corsair pass by. In the Rue de Rivoli, he spotted a house on fire. Firemen's helmets were blooming on the balconies and in the windows. Corsair Sanglot dashes down the corridor and up the collapsing staircase. On the fourth floor a woman was preparing to die. To clasp her in his arms and appear at the window takes a second. They leap into the void where they are caught by a blanket while, injured by a glancing cornice, Corsair Sanglot loses consciousness. The following morning, the sun shone on the infirmary where he rested in his bed. The rescued woman was pouring him some lemonade. He felt an almost sensual satisfaction at her presence near him, and also in the passage of her hands across his body, until the moment when the door of the English boarding-school opened. It was time to get up, thirty young girls and ten others a little older were hurrying about. The bath-sponge sent streams across their healthy shoulders and delicate skin. He paused to contemplate their almost boyish buttocks. Their sexes were still almost hairless but their breasts were charming delights, still undeformed by...

"Tell me that you love me!" gasped Louise Lame, lost.

"You bitch!" mocked the hero. "Love you? Ah! ha! you crazy old pile of shit, blessed name of filth upon filth!"

Then, getting up:

"What poem could move you more than that?"

Dumbfounded, Louise Lame passed from dream to dream. For a long time she denied herself the bony embraces of her companion. But their meeting was phenomenal. Bitterness rose in their souls. Ah! This wasn't love — the only valid reason for temporary slavery — but adventure itself, with all the obstacles of the flesh and all the odious enmity of matter.

Magnificent love, why must my language become so emphatic when I wish to evoke you? Corsair Sanglot had seized her round the waist and thrown her across the bed. He struck her. The sonorous rump had been soundly thrashed with the flat of his hand and the muscles would be blue the next day. He was almost choking her. Her thighs had been brutally forced apart.

This was not true.

Standing before the mirror, Corsair Sanglot completed his toilet. Comforting water streamed over his torso and the pinkish bar of soap was at the centre of this scene. Louise Lame, educated from picture postcards, saw the image of her sex there, martyred by indifference. The lather, the mask and the hands which were the hands of an apparition. Finally, the adventurer was ready to leave. Louise stood before the door.

"No, I won't let you go! I won't, I won't, I won't!"

He pushed her to one side with his hand and while she collapsed, bleeding, hair dishevelled, his steps faded down the stairs, like a scale played backwards on a piano by a learner: a little girl with braided hair, her fingers still red from the blows of the piano mistress's ruler.

In the corridor, the tread of the hotel bootboy coming to polish, pair by pair, the shoes with their Louis XV heels. What Father Christmas, whom we have been awaiting for centuries, will deposit love in these articles of footwear, objects of a daily and nocturnal ritual on the part of their owners in spite of our awaking disillusionment? What sinister demon amused itself polishing them brighter than any mirror with the intention of reproducing in them the reflection, transformed into negresses, of statuesque women moved to passion. Let them place their delicate white feet into these brodekins of moral torture! Their path will be forever strewn with the splintered glass of the broken philtres of interrupted dreams, the sharp pebbles of boredom. White feet going off in different directions, the chilblains of doubt will hurt you notwithstanding the burdensome prophesies of the local fortune-teller. According to one curious custom, it is necessary to go first to Nazareth in order to celebrate the anniversary of a divine birth. But as for the star...

The star is perhaps the pinkish cake of soap that Corsair Sanglot is holding in his foaming hand. It directs him more reliably than the water-diviner's rod, the trapper's trail, or any of the Michelin Guides. The humble but magnificent creatures of modern poetry set off on a walk through the streets.

And here are the groups of three enamel painters bearing gifts of red radiators to a future god where, high in the sky, the whiteness of an artificial dawn breaks over the whole world; and here are the long aprons of café waiters, some red, some white, placed under the protection of the archangel St Raphaël, performing miracles of equilibrium in order, at some undetermined date, to be able to pour the cordial which will resurrect the new redeemer.

From the top of the buildings, Bébé Cadum watches them go by. The night of his incarnation is approaching, when, streaming with snow and light, he will signal to his first disciples that the time has come to acknowledge the tranquil miracle of the washerwomen who turn the waters of the river blue and that of the god who may be seen beneath the soap-suds clinging to the body of a beautiful woman standing up in her bath-tub, queen and goddess of those glaciers of passion which gleam beneath a sweltering sun, a thousand times reflected, and ripe for death by sunstroke. Ah! If I myself should die, a second John the Baptist, let them make me a shroud of foaming soap-suds, evocative of love both by their texture and their smell.

Corsair Sanglot, guide in hand, followed the funeral procession, abandoning it at a certain point to go off in other directions. Quiet, deserted streets, sown with street-lamps, boulevards weighed down by Metro viaducts overhead, you also have seen him pass, the first of the Magi.

It was on the Isle of Swans, beneath the bridge at Passy, that Bébé Cadum was awaiting his guests. They behaved like perfect men of the world and the Eiffel Tower presided over the conventicle. Water flowed by.

The fish, dedicated for many ages and tempests to the cult of divine objects and celestial symbolism, jumped out of the water. For the same reason, the palm trees of the Jardin d'Acclimatation deserted their little alleys haunted by the peaceful elephants of childish sleep. The same thing happened to those, imprisoned in their pots of earth, which decorate the sitting-rooms of old ladies and brothels full of pillars. Unhappy women heard the prolonged crackings of the abandoned earthenware pots and the creeping of roots across the polished parquet floor; clubmen, forgetful of their gains or losses, slowly make their way home at dawn after a night of baccarat during which the numbers, like them, had followed each other into their traditional cells. They too were amongst the earliest of the faithful. Upon these melancholy foreheads, upon these eyes burning with fever, upon these ears still ringing with the last banco, upon these brains tormented by the absolute, by improbabilities and prophetic numbers, he extends his sovereignty. The air is full of the sound of closing windows and the weeping of their hasps. Bébé Cadum was born without the aid of parents, spontaneously.

On the horizon, a misty giant stretched and yawned. Bibendum Michelin[3] was preparing for a terrific struggle whose historian will be the author of these lines.

At the age of twenty-one, Bébé Cadum was strong and large enough to do battle with Bibendum. It began one morning in the month of June. A policeman strolling stupidly along the Champs-Élysées suddenly heard a tremendous noise in the sky. Then he was lost in the darkness as a soapy rain accompanied by thunder, lightning and strong winds lashed the city. In a moment the landscape became a fairyland. The roofs, covered in a light foam that was carried off flake by flake by the wind, were transformed into rainbows as the sun came out again. Innumerable rainbows sprang to life, frail and glowing faintly like the halos of young consumptives in the days when they were a necessary accessory to poetic creation. The passers-by stepped through a fragrant snow reaching up to their knees. Some began fights with the soap bubbles which the wind blew away, together with the innumerable windows reflected upon the sides of their transparent shells.

Then a charming madness settled on the town. The inhabitants tore off their clothes and ran through the streets, rolling on the soapy carpet. The Seine was full of lumpy, white sheets which clotted against the supports of the bridges and dissolved into milky clouds.

The conditions of existence were greatly changed with respect to their relations with material objects, but love continued to remain the privilege of a very small number of people who were prepared to chase after every adventure and risk the little time granted to mortals in the hope of finally meeting the adversary with whom one walks side by side, ever on the defensive and yet with utter abandon.

However, the fight between Bibendum and Bébé Cadum was not the only episode in the battle in which the modern archangel lost his lather like feathers.

Bibendum repaired to his retreat, where he proposed to compose his famous proclamation which later became known under the title of the *Paternoster of the False Messiah,** slipping and sliding around despite all his efforts to the contrary on the soapy lather.

Home at last, he immediately dictated his *Pater* and then, going out again, slipped upon the macadam, fell, died, and gave birth to an army of pneumatic tyres. It was their duty to continue the fight.

The encounter took place on a deserted plain. Bébé Cadum did not see the frightening troop of tyres arrive, bouncing and losing their shape, rolling quickly

*PATERNOSTER OF THE FALSE MESSIAH
         Bi   ben   dum
         Bé   bé
             Ca   dum

What is the goal of the usurper Bébé Cadum, who goes as far as to steal the name of the sole true Messiah?

Bébé is derived from *Biben*, for it is well known that the baby is fed by drinking (suckling); as for the syllable *Ca*, that is indicative of the bastardisation of *Bébé Cadum* from its etymological root *Bededum*, the putative son of *Bidendum*. The suppressed *n* tends to lead us to suppose that the site of his conception, following the example of Bacchus, was in the *groin* (thigh) of his father. However, he was, in fact, called into being in the completely normal manner, namely, by friction (*causa*) — the evidence for which he has been unable to suppress from his name. From this, in turn, is derived the property of transformation into lather when rubbed.

If those portions of the two names which reduplicate each other are suppressed, we are left with the following:

Bibe Bébé	cancel each other out by identical equivalence.
dum dum	are identical and cancel out by colliding with each other: *dum-dum* obviously represents the sound of thunder heard during battle.
N Ca	The close relationship between these two parts of the body is well known. Together they form *Can*, an abbreviation of *canon* (linked with the idea of thunder), and suggesting by its form the existence of *causa*.

along the streets to the terror of the pedal-cyclists and motorists who, shocked into silence, wondered what new miracle was responsible for bestowing on these elastic circles such autonomous agility.

The encounter took place on a deserted plain at the onset of sunset at five o'clock in the evening. The laughing Bébé Cadum stood out clearly against the burning blue sky and the dull red earth. The tyres coil around him like a reptile and immobilise him. Although a prisoner, Bébé Cadum will not relinquish his smile and allows himself to be thrown, despite his strength, into a dungeon. Bébé Cadum, or rather Christ, since we must call him by his true name in our own era, was thirty-three years old. The beard would have given his face a rather sinister appearance if it were not for the childlike grin which hovered on his lips. But let's not go into ancient history:

GOLGOTHA

The cross stands out at the top of the hill against the olive-green background of the sky. Weep, you virgins and apostles in the broad plain bustling with jousting windmills, the race of red and white cars on the silver-grey roads, the music of carousels with their wooden horses, the sharp reports from the shooting-galleries and the metallic revolutions of the wheel of fortune. The almost imperceptible movement of greasy poles bestows a heady vibration on this landscape in which the white tower of the helter-skelter and the mathematical motion of the steam-swing irresistibly symbolise the idea of passing time like a slow and majestic battleship upon a deep blue sea wrinkled by the occasional white crests of waves and a filigree of troughs under a light blue sky with, in the background, a beach cluttered with magnificent women in skin-coloured outfits, dumb sailors who wave their arms, adventurers in white canvas trousers haunted by the thought of the next steamship which will take them towards the casinos of South America and other more fatal liaisons, whilst, close to the shore, three wonderful lady swimmers in red bathing-costumes abandon themselves without restraint to the caprices of the gentle wavelets and are for the young poet squatting on a rock nothing less than the starting point for a dramatic adventure in which tempests and human passions combine to propel him amidst magical romances.

There, in a woody glade, let us review an entire company of firemen. There, in the sky, an aeroplane: it is on its way to Morocco or Russia; and there, a long way off, on the horizon, betrayed by white smoke and the strangely close sound of wheels on rails and axles, is a train heading full speed towards some port or harbour. In the tiny garden which surrounds his cottage, a meditative gardener waters the flowers. From the window of a school the voices of children escape: *We'll to the woods no more, the laurels have all been cut.*[4] At the window of a house a curtain flaps behind which two lovers are entwined on a perfectly ordinary bed as if they have been drowned. Two men are sitting in the grass, drinking an expensive red wine from the bottle. Three bulls in a meadow. The church weathervane. An aeroplane. Poppies.

Christ is finally worthy of his name: he is crucified upon a cross of oak decorated with tricolour pennants resembling a platform on 14 July. At its foot, a dozen or so musicians are playing catchy tunes on brass instruments. Some couples are dancing.

Upon little crosses, these also decorated with pennants, the two thieves are in the throes of death.

The priest leaves the church and returns to the presbytery. The swine.

Night falls.

The sky brightens violently with the glare of neon signs.

Christ's death-rattle beats time, following the rhythm of the orchestra.

The pennants on the cross flap joyfully.

The street-lamps light up.

IV. *The Illegal Gaming Squad*

Where is he in the days of slave-ships and caravels? He is as far away as a minute-glass in the balance of destiny.

The new Corsair, dressed in a dinner jacket, stands on the prow of his sleek yacht whose frothing wake imitates the princesses of the courts of yesteryear and which, during the course of its voyage, bumps against the victims of shipwrecks whose bodies have been adrift for weeks, or the mysterious chest carried from ocean to ocean by the gentle currents as the result of an attempted burglary on a transatlantic liner, or the corpse, wrapped in a stupid flag, of somebody who died before arriving at port, or the uncanny presence of the bony skeleton of a mermaid who died wearing her diadem of starfish while crossing the stormy waters lit up by the beam of a powerful lighthouse lost far from the shore and haunted by ghostly birds.

Because birds do have ghosts. At daybreak, these climb higher in the sky than larks and the sun softly filters through the hardly perceptible shadows of their wings. Happy is the consumptive sheltered in this manner! Her breath is supported by a soft pillow of still air and her fiancé, attentive to the tremor of her lips, will distinctly perceive the ripple of a smile. Occasionally, these great benevolent birds, dead since the final years of those geological periods in which man first appeared, feel their wings buckle beneath them, their agony gives rise to a tremendous eddy of wind and the grave-diggers leaning on their spades mentally calculate the number of corpses which still separate their sweating bodies from well-earned rest.

In the evening, these ghostly birds return to their nests in the transparent glaciers and the dusk is filled with the clamour of their dream-like flight and, from time to time, by their screams which long reverberate, without the assistance of audio equipment, in solitary souls.

The funereal remains of the mermaids, however, are not unaffected by these hourly migrations. With uneven stroke, their skeletons follow the courses of rivers upstream to their sources high in the mountains. Their calciferous remains are united in a mythological embrace with winged spectres, then the rivers flow ever more rapidly to carry them back to the sea.

When the bow of a boat encounters the skeleton of a mermaid, the water immediately becomes phosphorescent, then the froth of the waves solidifies in the shape of those pipes which are so renowned in the towns of the interior. The fishermen collect an enormous quantity in their nets until the mermaid's very skeleton is hauled up on deck.

Corsair Sanglot watched the reefs and the head cook's stories sail by. So fascinated was he by the movement of the water that he was hardly aware of the throb of the engine and the constant, steady churning of the propeller.

In the hold, coal was tossed on to the fire by the shovelful. Aware of the approaching hurricane, the grimy stokers redoubled their efforts. The warm coal burst into flames on their shovels, causing innumerable little blue flames to break out, flames which forever slumber in the hearts of sailors. As night falls in my blood-stained tale, as the stormy skies darken, the lights of St Elmo may be seen on the tops of the funnels.

So be it! Fall, artificial night of waking nightmares! Approach, mysterious storm! The boat is white against the dark grey cyclone. Great troughs stir the depths, seaweed appears on the surface of the water and, on the horizon, the ghostly ship rises from the sea, pilot-boat of the cataclysm.

Appear, lights of St Elmo! Appear, stage props of catastrophes: stifling weather, all too calm, copper-coloured skies, lead skies, ebony skies, pale sunbeams on hemlock-coloured waves, icebergs, waterspouts, maelstroms, reefs, flotsam, ground swell, stricken lifeboats, bottles in the sea.

I am waiting for her! Will she come? Every night for a year now I have been pacing up and down in front of her windows. When she is away, the place where she lives unceasingly projects on my closed eyes dreamy paths where I see her wander, the baccarat rooms as brilliant as a crystal chandelier, the hotel rooms with their view as thrilling as on the first morning of your stay. The love that overwhelms me, will it soon assume this woman's name?

Meanwhile, the vessel, buffeted by the high waves, was soon in danger. As a final misfortune the hold caught fire. The damp, hot coal-dust gave off a thick, suffocating smoke. Some jumped over the rails, others, despite the risk of the venture, took their chances in a tiny lifeboat lost in the mountainous seas.

Corsair Sanglot alone remained on board. The ship began to list. Corsair Sanglot noted the perfect lucidity of his thoughts which permitted him to remark numerous seemingly insignificant details. For example, the whistle of the wind brusquely changing to a bellow when — the funnels almost lying horizontally — it swept in as far as the fire-box; the strange sight of smoke coming out like a liquid and gently radiating across the undulating waves; the shifting stigmata of brightly-coloured oil on the surface of the water. Then a sizzling sound, which grew louder by the minute, signifying the inundation of the engines. They exploded in three different places at once amidst a fine spray, puffs of smoke and the birth of a funnel-shaped spout of water. The ship began to turn on its own axis and drive itself into the water at great speed. Wreckage began to float gently away until, suddenly, as if swallowed by an enormous mouth, the stricken vessel disappeared beneath the waves in an instant.

The boat sank some thirty metres or so before gradually coming to rest, hovering as if in a floating tomb. The tumult above could not reach it. Corsair

Sanglot opened his eyes. A submarine some distance away warily drifted past. Corpulent fish flitted back and forth. Tentacles of seaweed reached out even this far. Corsair Sanglot leaned forward to observe the sea bed. It looked a uniformly blackish yellow colour with the texture of blotting-paper or damp sand, and he guessed no deeper than a hundred metres.

Despite the darkness at these depths, the projected shadows of fish could be clearly seen as they flickered across the ocean floor. Corsair Sanglot prepared to go down. This was no easy matter since the reflection of his own image in the liquid element constantly got in the way of himself and his goal. But he closed his eyes, thrust his hands out violently before him, opened his eyes and grasped the hands of his reflection. The latter, as he retreated, reproduced on layer upon layer of water, rapidly dragged him to the bottom. He landed softly. Corsair Sanglot was buried up to his neck in a vast field of sponges. There must have been three or four thousand. Sea-horses, roused from their slumbers, rushed out from all sides at the same time as a gigantic illuminated candle of some marine species. By the light of this candle, the rippling sponges stretched away as far as the eye could see. Their papillae stood out in extraordinarily clear relief, and it was only with difficulty that Corsair Sanglot forced a passage between them. Finally, he reached the candle. It rose up in a sort of clearing called, according to a legend inscribed in the coral: "The Glade of the Mystical Sponge", where a herd of sea-horses was frolicking over a terrain composed of tiny black pebbles. The skeletons of a dozen mermaids were laid out side by side. Confronted by this cemetery, Corsair Sanglot felt a great relief. He contemplated this sacred place for a moment, then he went to sleep forever in the prairie of sponges. He could make out the uniforms of sailors of various nationalities, skeletons in dinner jackets and evening dresses.

But his spirit, like the trace left in the air by an aeroplane which is on fire, interpreted the landscape in its own fashion. It saw Christ accompanied by twelve mermaids on the way to meet His destiny; a blood-red cross standing out against an ebony sky, Egyptian papyri to the left and right, the ruins of a Greek column with His hat at its foot, telegraph lines on the horizon. It could still picture the diver who disdained pearl oysters in favour of the immense, foredoomed sponge which drew attention to itself in the blackness of the waters by a green halo.

But the marine candle was rapidly growing dim. The Corsair noticed that it was the starting point for a rainbow but instead of being seen from the inside of its circumference like a dome, this one appeared from the outside such that it stretched away like two horns or a crescent until the two most remote points on its surface where its spreading branches emerged rejoined each other high in the atmosphere and so became a source of delight for the ghostly birds, of wonder for the population and of sadness for the little boy blowing soap bubbles. The latter, as they rose in the air, had windows on their sides.

There was no longer any question of Corsair Sanglot remaining on the sea bed. As it burned, the candle formed enormous white stalactites which remained suspended for a moment before beginning their ascent.

He clung on to one of them and soon found himself swimming on the stillness of a wave, in sight of a boatless harbour, in the midst of an impressive silence.

Let her come, the one I shall love, instead of telling you wonderful stories (I was about to say boring stories). O nocturnal gratification, dawn anguish, distressful confidences, tenderness of desire, thrill of the fight, marvellous undulation of mornings after love-making.

You will read it or you won't, you will find it interesting or find it tedious, but moulded in a sensual prose I must express the love I have for my beloved. I see her, she approaches, she ignores me or pretends to ignore me. Even so, I can detect a certain warmth in her words and an allusiveness in one or two expressions.

I recall that last winter, a few months ago, she sang at a gathering of friends. She sang a sentimental love story that night and though I could not have cared less about the content of the song, her voice brought tears to my eyes. I can remember nothing more than the simple tune, which was a waltz, and one or two lines of the chorus in which the heroine declares her love.

She looked towards me at that point, but I could scarcely believe that this held any special significance. Do not tell me that she is beautiful, she is startling. Her glance made my heart beat faster, her absence fills all my senses.

Banality! Banality! That's the sensuous style for you! That's gushing prose for you. How far it is from the pen to the mouth. Let this novel in which, pretentiously, I wish to capture the healthy aspirations of love, be as absurd, as inadequate and as disappointing as you like. I feel a lump in my stomach when I am near her. I will make love in front of a crowd of three hundred without a thought, so unaware have I become of those around me. Be as banal as you like, tumultuous story.

I still believe in the marvellous when it concerns love, I believe in the reality of dreams, I believe in heroines in the night, in beauties of the night, forcing their way into hearts and into beds. You see, I hold out my arms for the gentle handcuffs, the handcuffs of the woman I have chosen, handcuffs of steel, handcuffs of flesh, fatal handcuffs. Young convict, it is time to print a number on your calico shirt and fetter your ankle with the heavy ball of your successive loves.

Corsair Sanglot reaches port. The breakwater is made of granite, the custom-house of white marble. And what silence. What was I talking about? About Corsair Sanglot. He reaches port, the breakwater is made of porphyry and the custom-house of molten lava… and what silence over it all.

Corsair Sanglot turns into an avenue, arrives at a square, and there is greeted by a life-sized statue of Jack the Ripper in suit and cocked hat. On the corner of every street are sponge shops proffering windows full of objects made of cork and ships in bottles. The windows of all the shops selling fire-alarms have been smashed. All the shutters are closed. On every rooftop, the platinum of lightning conductors shines and attracts larks. Over every roof preposterous oriflammes hover.

Corsair Sanglot walks through the deserted town.

How sweet, to bitter hearts, is solitude; how sweet, to souls filled with pride, is the sight of desolation. I rejoice in the slow promenade of our hero through the deserted town in which the statue of Jack the Ripper provides the only evidence that a population with highly-developed moral values once lived there. In this silent port, through these perfectly proportioned boulevards, in these magnificent public gardens walks the hero of a shipwreck and the hero of love. It is time for my beloved to make her appearance in this story.

As soon as she arrives, a supernatural being murmurs, as soon as she arrives, this magnificent town and your intrepid and indomitable hero will no longer understand why your imagination offers them such fleeting asylum.

Silence! She will come with her silk skirts, with her cherry-coloured bodices, her fawn boots, orange make-up, she will come in the manner in which I love her and we shall depart freely towards adventure.

Blessed be that galley ship! How beautiful will be the shores we shall glimpse! How luxurious will be the chain that links us! How liberating that ship will seem!

From square to square, Corsair Sanglot arrives in front of a cabinet-maker's shop. Nothing but rosewood sideboards and oak chairs. For a long moment he is lost in corridors in which brand new dining-rooms give way to equally new bedrooms. The monotonous procession of carefully polished parquet tiles intoxicates him. From time to time a lift shaft reveals its suspicious, open well. On the ceiling there are old-fashioned chandeliers laden with crystal which hang down like Canaan grapes and reflect to infinity the unexpected visitor. When at dusk he left, the public fountains filled the streets with imaginary mermaids. They entwined themselves, turning and dragging themselves to the very feet of the corsair. Dumb, they implored the conqueror for the song which would restore their lower limbs, but dry of throat he did not disturb the streets and sonorous walls with his voice because his clear eyes, clearer perhaps than the eyes of reality, could discern beyond the desert and the inhabited areas the shadow of the dress of my beloved whom I have never stopped thinking about even as my pen, animated in part by itself and animated in part by all the rest, flies into the lambent paper sky. My pen is a wing and every word, borne by it and by its shadow on the paper, rushes towards either catastrophe or apotheosis.

I have just spoken of the magical phenomenon of writing considered as an organic and optical manifestation of the marvellous. With respect to the chemistry, the alchemy of this handwriting, whose beauty is appreciated by nobody, and, I insist, from a solely calligraphical point of view (my apologies for any element of repetition which might or might not have crept in here), I advise the seasoned observers of atomic structure to enumerate the ocular drops of water through which these words have passed before returning in a malleable form to confront my memory and count the drops of blood or the fragments of drops of blood consumed by this writing.

Corsair Sanglot was still walking.

Here, at last, is the woman whose coming I have announced, marvellous adventures will link them together. They are going to bump into whatever.

She is wearing cherry-coloured silk, she is tall, she is, she is, what exactly is she like?

She is here.

I can see her in every detail of her splendid nature. I am going to touch her, stroke her.

Corsair Sanglot undertakes to, Corsair Sanglot begins to, Corsair Sanglot, Corsair Sanglot.

The woman I love, the woman, ah! I was going to write her name. I was going to write "I was going to write her name."

Count, Robert Desnos, count the number of times you have used the words "marvellous", "magnificent"...

Corsair Sanglot no longer walks around the shop of reproduction furniture.

The woman that I love!

V. *The Bay of Famine*

Ebony boat under way for the North Pole, death now presents itself in the guise of a circular and frozen bay, without penguins, without seals, without bears. I know the agony of a ship caught in the ice floes, I know the frozen death-rattle and the pharaonic death of the Arctic and Antarctic explorers, with their green and red angels and scurvy and their skin burnt by the cold. From one of the capitals of Europe, an ever-growing newspaper carried by the south wind rapidly makes its way towards the Pole, its two sheets like two enormous, funereal wings.

Nor do I forget the telegrams of condolence nor the idiotic anecdote of the national flag planted in the ice, nor the repatriation of bodies on gun carriages.

Stupid evocation of the desert life. Whether the deserts be made of ice or of porphyry, located on the ship or in the train, lost in the crowd or in space, this sentimental image of universal disorder does not move me.

Her lips bring tears to my eyes. She is there. Her words strike my temples with deadly hammer blows. In my imagination her thighs lure me unthinkingly onwards. I love you yet you pretend to ignore me. I would like to believe that you pretend to ignore me or rather that your gestures are full of allusions. The most ordinary expressions contain moving hidden meanings when you speak to me.

You told me you were sad. Would you have said this to someone who didn't care for you? You said the word "love" to me. How could you have failed to notice my emotion? How could you not have intended to provoke my feelings?

If you do not know me, you whose presence is not even essential to me, it can only mean that this calendar has been badly printed. Your photographs on my walls and the bitter memories that our meetings have impressed upon my heart have only a paltry rôle in my love! You figure large in my dreams, ever-present, alone on the stage yet destitute of any rôle.

I encounter you rarely on my path. I am of an age when one begins to contemplate one's emaciated fingers, and at which youth is so full, so real that it cannot be long before it begins to fade. Your lips bring tears to my eyes; you sleep naked in my brain and I dare not rest.

And, what's more, I have had enough, don't you understand, of talking aloud of you.

Far from our secrets, Corsair Sanglot continues on his way in the abandoned city. It comes to pass, because everything comes to pass, that he arrives in front of a new building, the Mental Asylum.

To enter is no more than a formality for him. The doorman shows him to a clerk. His name, age and desires noted down, he takes possession of a charming little cell painted bright red.

As soon as he has passed the last door of the asylum, he is approached by several men of genius.

"Come in, my son, come into this place reserved for mortified souls and let the soothing spectacle of our seclusion prepare your pride for the future glory reserved for it by God in His paradise of satin and sugar. Far from the vain sounds of the world, patiently admire the contradictory sight that the absolute divinity imposes on your meditations and, rather than bathing in the endless shape of the Lord, let yourself be overwhelmed by the victorious atmosphere of His battles with the small but numerous miasma of society; let the very savour of God agitate your mouth devoted to fasting, to prophecy and to communion with the universal provider, let your dazzled eyes forget even the memory of material objects in order to contemplate the radiant shafts of His faith, let your hand distinctly feel the brush of archangels' wings, let your ear absorb mysterious, revelatory voices. And if this advice seems to you corrupted with a satanic sensuality, just remember that it is not true that the senses are the slaves of matter. They belong to the spirit, they serve the spirit alone and it is only through them that you can hope to experience the final ecstasy. Look into yourself and admit the excellence of the orders issued by sensuality. Never will they attempt to do other than identify the immaterial; in defiance of painters, sculptors, musicians, perfumiers and chefs, they seek only the absolute idea. Each of these artists merely addresses the sense that suits him most whereas, in order to attain the supreme states of bliss, it is necessary to cultivate all of them. A materialist is someone who claims to abolish these wonderful senses! In this way he deprives himself of the efficacious assistance of ideas since abstract ideas do not exist. Ideas are concrete, every one of them. Once emitted, they correspond to a creation, to some point or other on the spectrum of the absolute. Deprived of sense, the wretched ascetic is no more than a skeleton surrounded by flesh. The latter and his kin are devoted to inviolable ossuaries. Thus, you should cultivate your senses either to achieve supreme bliss or ultimate torment, both of which are enviable since they are supreme and within your reach."

Thus spoke a pseudo-Lacordaire.[5]

And prove to me, if you can, that it wasn't the real one. It was two o'clock in the afternoon. The sun split open and a shower of compasses crashed to the ground: magnificent compasses made of nickel and each one of them pointing to the same north.

The same north where Albert's team was now in the process of slowly dying among the crystals. Years later, some fishermen from the Sunda Islands recovered a barrel, a vestige of the expedition, a smelly, white barrel of salt. One of the fishermen felt the attraction of mystery growing inside him. He leaves for Paris. He becomes an employee at a special club.

The rain of compasses slowly comes to an end. Instead of a rainbow, Joan of

Arc-of-the-Rainbow appears. She comes to frustrate the intrigues of a future reactionary. Every army is the product of tendentious manuals, Joan of Arc has come to combat Joan of Arc-of-the-Rainbow. The latter, a pure heroine dedicated by sadism to war, summons to her assistance numerous Théroigne de Méricourts,[6] Russian terrorists in tight, black satin dresses, impassioned criminals. The female pearl-diver sees the eyes of the men listening to her grow round. Intoxicated, she is caught in her own game. Her lover, in a fishing-boat, participates in the same dream.

At that moment, the pearl-diver, drawing a revolver from her bodice (where the besotted guard their love letters) said: "I love you, O my darling lover! and today is the day that I alone have just chosen to offer you the yawning wound of my sex and the bleeding wound of my heart." And with these words she presses the gun against her breast and, as a tiny cloud of blue smoke rises into the air with the report, slumps forward.

The auditorium empties in silence. A man in a dress coat is still garnering a kiss from the mouth of an adorable woman. Joan of Arc-of-the-Rainbow, her breast exposed, astride an unsaddled white horse, rides around Paris. And it is in this manner that petards made of dynamite destroy the stupid effigy — made of the same copper used to manufacture saucepans in the Rue des Pyramides — of St Augustine along with the church (one less!) as an additional bonus.

Joan of Arc-of-the-Rainbow, triumphing over calumny, yields to love.

Albert's expedition with its masts crowned by an oriflamme is now at the centre of a pyramid of ice. A looming sphinx of ice provides the finishing touch to the landscape. From the burning sands of Egypt to the irresistible Pole a miraculous current is established. The sphinx of ice speaks to the sphinx of the sands.

Sphinx of ice. — Let him arise, the lyrical Bonaparte. From the summit of my pyramid forty geological periods survey not a handful of conquerors, but the world. Sailing-boats and steam-boats, fine camels advance towards me, never reaching me, and I persist in contemplating in the four perfectly polished facets of this translucent monument the prismatic decomposition of the aurora borealis.

Sphinx of the sands. — The time is now approaching! We already suspected the existence of a polar Egypt whose pharaohs wear not the scarab of the sands on the crest of their helmets but the sturgeon. From the depths of a six-month night, a fair-haired Isis arises astride a white bear. Glistening whales will destroy with a flick of their tail the floating cradle of the Moses of the Eskimos. Memnon's giants will challenge the giants of the Memoui. Crocodiles are changing into seals. Before long, holy revelations will disclose the great algebraic signs necessary to join the stars together.

Sphinx of ice. — Pains for the body, words for thought! The polar riddle which I propound for adventurers is not a solution. Every riddle has twenty solutions. Words proclaim indifferently the for and the against. There is still no possibility of catching a glimpse of the absolute.

The pearl-diver, covered in blood — did I not intend to kill her? but she survived this mental attack — the pearl-diver, all bloody, sees Joan of Arc-of-the-Rainbow, her sister, enter the room. On the useless plinths of the statue of Jeanne de Lorraine,[7] gigantic squids of mineral coal are erected. Miners will go there to lay wreaths and a tiny Davy lamp will burn night and day in memory of the hirsute sex of the true adventuress.

Corsair Sanglot, whom I left in his charming cell, falls asleep.

An ebony angel sits down by his bed-head, switches off the light, and opens the grammar of dreams. Lacordaire speaks:

"Just as in 1789 the absolute monarchy was overthrown, in 1925 we must overthrow the absolute deity. There is something stronger than God. We must draft a Declaration of the Rights of the Soul, we must liberate the spirit, not by subjugating it to materialism but by refusing henceforth to subjugate it to materialism!"

Joan of Arc-of-the-Rainbow, after walking for years, arrives before the sphinx of ice with *Journey to the Centre of the Earth* under her arm.

Riddle

"What is it that climbs higher than the sun and descends lower than fire, that is more liquid than the wind and harder than granite? "

Without thinking, Joan of Arc-of-the-Rainbow replies:

"A bottle."

"Why?" asks the sphinx.

"Because I wish it."

"Fine, pass by, Oedipus in flesh and idea."

She passes. A trapper approaches her, loaded with sealskins. He asks her if she knows Matilde, but she does not. He gives her a homing-pigeon and each of them follow divergent paths.

In the laboratory of celestial ideas, a pseudo-Solomon of Cos puts the finishing touches to his plans for a perpetual motion machine. His system, based on the movement of the tides and the sun, occupies forty-eight sheets of Canson paper. At the very moment I write these lines the inventor is extremely busy covering the forty-eighth sheet with tiny triangular flags and asymmetrical stars. It is not long before a result is achieved.

As the eleventh hour approaches to the accompaniment of a bubbling alchemical solution, a slight sound is heard at the window. It opens. Night sweeps into the laboratory in the guise of a pale woman naked under a large astrakhan coat. Her close-cropped blonde hair creates a hazy luminosity around her delicate face. She places her hand on the engineer's forehead and he feels a mysterious fountain cascade under the defensive wall of his migraine-racked temples.

It would take a migration of albatrosses and pheasants to soothe away these headaches. They would spend an entire hour in the surrounding countryside before swooping down into the fountain.

But the migration does not happen. The waters of the fountain flow undisturbed.

Night departs, leaving a bouquet of water-lilies on the single bed. In the morning, the warder sees the bouquet. He interrogates the madman who makes no reply and from that time forth, his arms in a strait-jacket, the unfortunate man will never leave his cell again.

By dawn, Corsair Sanglot has already taken leave of this contemptible place.

Joan of Arc-of-the-Rainbow, the pearl-diver, and Louise Lame find themselves in a drawing-room. It is possible to see the Eiffel Tower through the window, grey against a cinder sky. On a mahogany desk, a bronze paper-weight in the shape of a sphinx stands next to a perfectly white glass sphere.

What do you do if there are three of you and no one else? Take off your clothes. The pearl-diver's dress falls to the ground in a single movement leaving her in her underwear. Her breasts and thighs are partially revealed beneath her short, white chemise. She yawns and stretches as Louise Lame carefully unhooks her tailor-made suit. The languor of the exercise makes the spectacle all the more exciting. A breast pops out and disappears again. Then she is naked too. As for Joan, she has already torn off her blouse and stockings.

All three admire themselves in a cheval-glass and night, the colour of glowing embers, covers them with the reflected glow of the street-lamps, hiding their passionate embrace on the sofa. The group is nothing more than pale shapes animated by sudden movements, a heaving mass breathing with one breath.

Corsair Sanglot walks beneath their window. He glances up at it distractedly as he has looked up at other windows. He wonders where his three companions could be and continues on his way. His shadow, projected by a car's headlights, rotates on the ceiling of the drawing-room like the hand of a watch. The three women contemplate it for a moment. Long after he has gone, they wonder what could have produced the unease which still torments them. One of them pronounces the Corsair's name.

"Where is he now? Dead, perhaps?" and late into the night they dream by the fireside.

Albert's expedition has been discovered by some whale-hunters. The ship caught in the ice contains nothing but corpses. A flag planted in the ice floe testifies to the work of the unfortunate sailors. Their remains are transported back to Oslo (formerly Christiana). Two cruisers pay them a final tribute. A company of marines keeps vigil over their bodies until the arrival of the battleship which will transport them back to France.

The mental asylum, white in the early morning sunshine, with its high walls overhung by calm, slender trees, resembles the tomb of King Mausolus.[8] And this is how the Seven Wonders of the World occur. They have been sent from time immemorial to madmen who fall victim to human despotism. Here is the Colossus of Rhodes. The asylum does not even reach up to its ankles. He is standing, feet apart. The Pharos of Egypt, in a frock-coat, peeps into every window. Great red beams sweep the city which is deserted despite the tramways, three million inhabitants and a well-organised police force. From a barracks, reveille sounds hollow and cruel, while the allegorical crescent of the moon finally dissolves on the line of the horizon.

A powerful old man, with a high forehead and stern eyes, wanders about the gardens of the Champ-de-Mars. He makes his way to the open metal pyramid of the tower. He goes up. The guard watches the old man lose himself in deep thought. He leaves him alone. Then the old man climbs over the balustrade, hurls himself into space and what happens next is of no further concern to us.

There are moments in life when the reason for our acts appears to us in all its fragility.

I breathe, I look, I am unable to confine my thoughts to an enclosed arena. They insist on leaving a wake of intersecting furrows.

How can you expect that corn, the principal preoccupation of the people I despise, will grow there?

But Corsair Sanglot, the music-hall chanteuse, Louise Lame, the polar explorers and the madmen, inadvertently united on the arid plain of a manuscript, will hoist to the top of the white masts the black flags signalling the presence of yellow fever in vain if they have not previously — ghosts flying out of the still night of the ink-well — abandoned the preoccupations dear to the one who, on this perfect liquid night, does nothing except make stains with his fingers, stains appropriate for leaving fingerprints on the painted walls of dreams and in that way capable of leading into error the ridiculous seraphim of logical deduction, persuaded as they are that only a mind fully familiar with majestic shadows could leave a tangible trace of its indecisive nature as it flees from the approach of danger like day or awakening, and far from imagining that the work of the book-keeper and that of the poet eventually leaves the same stigmata on paper and that only the shrewd eye of adventurers of the mind is capable of making the distinction between the lines devoid of mystery of the former and the prophetic — and perhaps, though unbeknown to him, divine — grimoire of the latter, because deadly plagues are only tempests caused by the clash of hearts and it is advisable to confront them with individual ambition and a mind free of the stupid hope of transmuting paper into a mirror by means of magical and effective writing.

VI. *Polemic Against Death*

Louise Lame's body is placed in a coffin and the coffin on a hearse. This ludicrous vehicle makes its way to the cemetery at Montparnasse. After crossing the river, passing a row of houses, negotiating tram-stops which obstruct the road, passers-by doff their hats, the differing rate of progress of the *cortège* is such that the mourners are either bumping into each other's backs or lagging behind, the conversation of the undertakers…

1st Undertaker. — Where I come from there was a great house. The house and the person who lived there could pick flowers at their leisure from all the surrounding countryside, so great were the privileges conferred by the house on its inhabitants. But the wave and the plinth of statues care more about other things: the one for the salt which piles up in cones in the artificial marshes; the other for the homing-pigeon flying overhead in the sky with a love letter under its wing. "Dearest Matilde, the enormous otters of the polar regions and the wolves wrapped up warmly in their fur throw themselves at our rifles when I utter your name. I have found a Calvary in the middle of the steppe. When I touched the Christ, he fell to pieces like a prehistoric mammoth frozen in the ice and the dogs which pull my sledge devoured him. And before they had even been to confession too. But then there isn't a confession for dogs. They were starving. My dearest, darling Matilde, your lover, your lover…" They were not concerned with flowers. They dug a tremendous subterranean cave beneath their home in an attempt to reach the sea, they cleared a carefully buttressed passage through the soft earth, the chalky layers, fragments of fossils, underground caverns, caverns frequently traversed by a crystal clear stream, bristling with stalactites and stalagmites, occasionally decorated with prehistoric drawings or cluttered with bones which were almost impossible to identify, without fear of the almost complete darkness which reigned there, nor of premature burial. After six years' work, they reached the sea. The light and the waves gushed in together and drowned them. A salt-water geyser which sprang up on the spot of the abandoned house is the only remaining trace of this adventure.

2nd Undertaker. — The coffee mill whirred in the cook's hands. Then in the quiet of the orchard the heart-rending cry of the caretaker was heard: "Madame is dying! Madame is dead!" The poor woman was indeed dead, in the lap of luxury: on a pillow of carrots and in a shroud of peach blossom. And in the mourning household the sound of the coffee mill whirring in the rough hands of the invisible cook in the blue apron has been heard ever since and the lover lacking courage and the priest of ill-omen have not passed the closed windows with impunity.

3rd Undertaker. — When he got a rise, the Wandering Jew bought a bicycle. He went up and down the roads, especially those which followed the crests of hills, where the sun projected and enlarged the wheels in circles of spinning shadows which passed in a sinister manner over the fields and hamlets. From his passage numerous tranquil spots were born. The signal on the railway line stirred slowly. As dusk fell a far-off shepherdess lifted her skirt higher than her breasts and exposed herself on the roadside to the surprise of a perplexed tourist. There he is, the Wandering Jew, going across the Place de l'Opéra.

4th Undertaker. — Two trees secretly embrace one night. At daybreak, each regains the narrow territory defined by their roots and, a short while later, a hunter comes to a halt there, astonished by the signs left by their movement. He dreams of the fabulous animal which in his mind must be responsible. He carefully loads his rifle and prowls the countryside for the rest of the day. The only animal he manages to kill is a raven which he does not even bother to pick up. As night falls, the raven comes to its senses. It climbs into the air, spreading its wings. The next day is foggy with a red sun like the cross-section of a tomato; the day after is foggy with a faint sun like a pale egg yolk; and so on for three months until there is eternal night. The peasants set the forest on fire so as to be able to see. Clouds of ravens flee into the air. The following day, daylight, but there is a little pile of embers in the place where the trees had been, thirty-three little ravens in the ploughed field, two pale grey wings on the back of the hunter. Two wings which grow darker every evening and shed less light with every morning. Eventually, he becomes the ebony archangel whose gun strikes terror into the breasts of the wicked. Then, one hot midday, his wings begin to beat without his intending. They carry him off high into the air and far away. Since then, throughout his native region, no one has engraved their initials into the trunks of old oak trees.

The procession was going down an avenue as the fourth undertaker finished his story.

To hell with Louise Lame's hearse, Louise Lame's corpse and her coffin, and the passers-by who raise their hats and those following the *cortège*. What do I care about this foul carcass and this carnival procession? There is never a day in which the ridiculous image of death does not intervene in the ever-changing backdrop of my dreams. Physical death makes hardly any impression on me since I live in eternity.

Eternity is the sumptuous theatre where liberty and love each struggle to possess me. Eternity surrounds me on all sides like an enormous egg-shell and it is here that liberty, that beautiful lioness, metamorphoses herself according to her pleasure. There she is, a conventional storm under motionless clouds. There she is again, a virile woman in a Phrygian cap, in the gallery of the Convention and on the Terrasse des Feuillants.[9] But although a woman, is she also that marvellous (once again that word of predestiny in the Olympia of my nights), pliable woman, already seduced, who is even now in love? Love with its primitive breasts and cold throat. Love with its imprisoning arms, love with its tumultuous wakes, the two of us, in a bed covered with lace.

I could never choose other than to remain here under the translucent cupola of eternity.

The family vault is to be found at ground level in the shadow cast by the tomb of Dumont d'Urville.[10] But do not think that the latter's funereal monument, a handsome red-brick cone reminiscent of those of the South Sea Islands, would keep me in this place furnished with objects which for the most part mark the limits of their destiny. The walls of the cemetery no more delineate the bounds of my wholly imaginary existence than the ocean or the desert or the glaciers. And that material figure, the skeleton of the dance of death, may knock on my window and enter my bedroom whenever he pleases. He will find a robust opponent who will laugh off his embrace. Coiners of epitaphs, monumental masons, funeral orators, wreath-sellers, your entire sepulchral crew is incapable of interrupting the sovereign flight of my projected life, lacking both rhyme and reason, further than the ends of the earth, Jehoshaphat's fairs or biographies. Louise Lame's hearse may wend its way through Paris without incident, I shall not raise my hat to it as it passes. I have a rendezvous with Louise Lame tomorrow and nothing will prevent me from being there. She will be there too. Pale beneath a wreath of clematis perhaps, but real and tangible and ready to subject herself to my will.

Destiny does not betray my trust.

Louise Lame dead comes to me and none of those we meet can detect any change in her. Only a barely perceptible odour of the grave was mingled with the ambergris perfume she was wearing, an odour that I quickly recognised, having smelled it many times close to the crumpled sheets seen at dawn like the confused motion of the morning tide frozen on the turn or rather, because of the contradictory ripples formed by the impact of the limbs of a corpse thrown into a liquid, for example, a man into a river, with, if you like, a stone around his neck: concentric rings. Because everything lends itself to the evocation of death. Ever since the discovery of the bottle, human corpses buried since the far-off days of the sphinx in the balsamic wrappings of the Egyptians, to the pen-holder which, should it be black, is a raven flying so fast that it transforms itself into a thin line before colliding with the church weathercock, the pen has dominated the cemetery with the written word which finally dries out on the white marble surface of the paper. If it is red, it is the physical flame of a technicolour hell or the ideal one of a crematorium. A hat, that is the halo of the saints or the crowns of the final day on which the kings, in disobedience to the signal given by the star, went — with their derisory symbols: porcelain diadems, caps of artificial pearls and steel wire and the thousand regrets and the "to my lover" instead of footmen — in the opposite direction to ask of the earth what belongs to the soul.

Similarly, is not the bottle a woman stretched out at the moment of orgasm, and an insensitive dreamer in the breeze and a teat for the lover's mouth and a phallus. And the pen-holder too, obscene and symbolic in the poet's hand, and the hat cleft like a sex or round like a croup. All these images bring about a levelling of the spirit. Are they not equal, all these elements comparable with the same accessory? Death is to life and to love, as day is to night.

Hocus pocus, the eternal mainspring of mathematics and metaphysics! Nothing is capable of contradicting itself and I heartily mistrust those who hesitate between the two burning poles of thought on the cold equator of scepticism. Commonplaces which shock the highest beliefs, by what abuse of confidence do you cite your authority to live meanly? While the foolish wind which animates you urges that it is so good to let yourself go.

My spirit yields to it like a bullet to a rifle. How they make me laugh all those who, during this tempest, pretend to do otherwise than make the desperate gestures of windmills, the contortions of kites, the arbitrary motions of wings, those who claim that they are helmsmen capable of reaching port, those for whom doubt is not a synonym for anxiety, those who smile delicately!

The goal? But that is the wind itself, the tempest, for whatever landscape they uproot, are they not intangible and logical?

All men are imbeciles. Having lowered the boat's sails on the same principle as the tornado, they believe getting shipwrecked is less logical than sailing.

What contempt I have for those who do not even know of the wind's existence. Better to deny it while remaining completely in its power.

"But death?"

"Is good for you."

VII. *Revelation of the World*

Towards the middle of the afternoon, Corsair Sanglot found himself (or found himself again) on a boulevard lined with plane trees. He would have walked a good deal further if a naked woman lying on the pavement had not attracted his attention. Once upon a time, Louise Lame had covered his throat with kisses which the populace found scandalous. Then the adjacent streets had pulled them in opposite directions. They never saw each other again. As for this naked corpse lying in a district which could only be somewhere like Invalides or Monceau, judging by the gilded dome rising above the roof-tops of modern buildings, no one was able to explain its presence there. Anyone but Corsair Sanglot would have continued on his way after a moment's hesitation, but taking the sky and the trees and the impassive macadam as witness to the fact that this woman was adorable, despite the signs of *rigor mortis* setting in, he felt the birth of a peculiar emotion in his heart, that which the meeting of love and death alone is able to arouse in a respectable soul. Landscape of emotions, superior region of love where we construct tombs forever unoccupied, at the moment the final physical metamorphosis is invoked before him, man does not fail to assume a certain nobility.

Corsair Sanglot had no need to go any further before the cypress avenues of the solitary dream encountered the soles of his imagination.

He noticed a granite building situated on the pavement close by the beautiful corpse. On the second-floor balcony a sign, similar in style and shape (golden letters on a black background) to that of a milliner's, reflected a negro sun:

À LA MOLLE BERTHE

Corsair Sanglot did not hesitate. He went down the corridor. The concierge, a beautiful mermaid, was engaged in changing her scales, according to the fashion of the season. Everywhere in this lodge furnished with a table, a sideboard and an Henri II wall-clock, there was a snowstorm of green and white scales. The metamorphosis was soon complete, and the mermaid flaunted a magnificent tail of white scales which resembled wool. But the Corsair quickly climbed the stairs.

The mermaid raised her webbed white hand in the direction of the staircase.

"Beware, Corsair Sanglot, pillager of medusas, ravisher of starfish, murderer of sharks! No one can resist my gaze with impunity."

On reaching the second floor, the young man knocked at the door of an apartment. A tall footman in gold-trimmed livery opened the door and showed him into a vast reception room. He took a seat in a leather armchair not far from a small bridge table. The flunkies of the Sperm Drinkers' Club danced attendance upon him. Having selected a choice vintage, a Senegalese sperm from the year of the wreck of *The Medusa*, Corsair Sanglot lit a cigarette.

The Sperm Drinkers' Club is an immense organisation. It employs women the whole world over to masturbate the most handsome men. A special squad is dedicated to finding the female elixir. Patrons prize equally a certain mixture to be found in the appropriate receptacle after wondrous onslaughts have occurred. Each harvest is preserved in a tiny phial of crystal, glass or silver which is then carefully labelled and dispatched to Paris. The club's agents are incredibly dedicated. Some have even died in the course of their perilous enterprises, and each of them pursues their goal with passion. Better still is he who will come up with the most inspired idea. One gathers the sperm of a condemned man who has been guillotined in France or hanged in England, the manner of death determining the taste of the respective emissions, be it water-lily or walnut. Another assassinates young girls and fills his phials with the seminal fluid which their lovers cannot help but release while in the grip of the tragic shock which the imparting of the terrible news causes them. Yet another, posted in an English boarding-school, garners the evidence of a young girl's excitement when, having been overtaken by puberty without her teachers noticing, she is obliged, in reparation for a venial sin, to receive, skirt up and drawers down, a spanking and a caning in the presence of her female class-mates and perhaps even a schoolboy, there by chance, the god of amatory pleasures. The founders of the club, the last occultists, held their first meeting towards the beginning of the Restoration.[11] And since then, from father to son, the association has perpetuated itself under the twin aegis of love and liberty. A poet long ago lamented the fact that the club had not been founded in the closing days of antiquity. Had that been the case they might have been able to preserve the sperm of both Christ and of Judas and, over the course of the centuries, that of Charles Stuart of England, of Ravaillac[12] and the passionate tears of Mlle de Lavallière[13] as she was whisked from Chaillot at a sensuous trot in her horse-drawn carriage and those of Théroigne de Méricourt on the Terrasse des Feuillants and the wonderful sperms which flowed during those violent years on the platforms of the Revolution as surely as the blood with which they mingled. Another permanently regretted the loss of the divine potion constituted by the malmsey in which the Duke of Clarence drowned.

The members of the club adore the sea. The phosphorous odour which it exudes makes them light-headed and, amongst the flotsam cast up on the shores, the wreckage of boats, fish bones, relics of submerged cities, they find the atmosphere of love and that breathlessness which, at the same time, carries confirmation to our ears of the concrete existence of the imaginary, mixed pell-mell with the particular crunch of drying seaweed, the emanation of that magnificent aphrodisiac, marine amber, and the plash of white-crested waves against the sex and thighs of bathers at the precise moment when, having finally reached their waists, they slap their bathing-costumes against their flesh. How long had Corsair Sanglot been drinking? Night was falling! A considerable number of phials lay broken at his feet as the first star came out, from the frosted glass of the Senegalese to the amber glass of the Eskimo whose essence cannot withstand daylight, accustomed as they are to making love only during the six months of polar darkness.

Just like the parasol which, capriciously raised, suddenly protects the beautiful lone swimmer who has survived the catastrophe until the moment when she faints from sun-stroke at midday before reaching a land where she may await rescue, Bébé Cadum, erected on the roof of the house opposite, caught the drinker's eye.

"Just imagine, sir," his neighbour said to him, "the stupefaction of the young girl, taken unawares and tied up and undressed, in front of whom naked men and women assume indescribable postures, while a handsome native of the Sunda Islands strokes her in the most intimate manner as she holds a champagne glass beneath her. It is this stupefaction which gives the liquid its distinctive taste of sea-pine."

"Personally," replied another imbiber, "I prefer male sperm to female."

Here is a curious conversation which took place under the influence of sperm.

"Semale femen?"

"More like sole."

"Soles? Solar days? Time and space. The only connection between them is that of hatred and wings."

"Sorrel is indeed a matchless dish, a dish fit for a king."

"Menses, trash."

"Word for word, work for work, turf for turf, that's how life goes."

"The hour finally tolls."

"There trolls the aulder."

"Whose troll?" asked Corsair Sanglot.

"Faint heart never laid a wan fairy."

"Vulgar pseudo-intellectuals."

"At this very moment, a corridor of wind and storm carries off a minister. His Légion d'Honneur flaps in the air for a moment like a swallow then subsides. A second and a third minister follow him. Like several goldfish in an aquarium seducing a ladybird, the despair of these animals makes for a curious tragedy, for they were intended to love each other but, separated by a glass partition, turn their backs on each other."

A new arrival. — "Just imagine, gentlemen, the panic of a strong, sturdy woman, proud and haughty, who has been completely overpowered and who is being tenderly sodomised by a young man while still half-dressed. Her skirt and petticoat are rolled up between her stomach and her rump. Her cami-knickers have been pulled down to her knees, her wrinkled silk stockings constitute a charming disarray. From the front, her clothes hang almost normally. But there, at the place where they are lifted up, can be seen traces of bare flesh and, in the shadow of rumpled underwear, one can detect the shape of her buttocks. The young man, having lubricated the firm flesh, parts the buttocks. He slowly penetrates her, gently and with a regular movement. A fresh emotion seizes hold of the victim, her wetness is a clear sign of her pleasure. A young girl delicately harvests those sacred tears with a silver spoon and places them in a tiny pot made of red stoneware, then, having slipped almost entirely between the couple's legs thanks to her small size, she does not miss any of the seminal fluid which froths from around the pulsating member. When love, magnificent tango, has become a tempest of cries and sobs, she gathers from around the edge of the rim a warm, sweetly-scented snow; when the orifice is completely clean, she places her mouth against it, a tiny, red suction disc. She breathes in deeply and mixes it intimately with her saliva, which likewise finds its way into the earthenware pot. To finish, the kneeling woman allows the child to collect her tears of shame, anger, joy and exhaustion."

"Thus have we wished the marvellous grape to be pressed. Our passion is totally devoid of idolatry. Go on and laugh, you deophagous monks and nuns, imbecile freemasons. For an instant our imagination discovers in this feast a reason to rise higher than the eternal snows. Hardly has the marvellous savour invaded our palates, hardly are our senses thrown into turmoil than a tyrannical image replaces that of love's ascension: that of an interminable and monotonous road, of an immense cigarette emitting a haze which blurs the towns and cities, that of twenty hands holding twenty different cigarettes, that of a plump mouth."

And Corsair Sanglot cries aloud:

"I brood over the imperious mysteries of language. The word '*hafnal*' which is to be found in the *Chanson du dékioskoutage*[14] and which means 'arse', derives from the English expression *half and half*. The superlative of the word *Present* is *President* — he who is and who is above others. The word *ridicule* is a corruption of *ride-cul*,[15] a corruption which is easily explained if you think that when you laugh you have to open your mouth, which gives rise to a surplus of skin which is transmitted by way of minute wrinkles to the opposite orifice. It is only logical, therefore, that ridicule provokes laughter."

This speech broke the silence in the minds of the members of the Sperm Drinkers' Club. Bébé Cadum had a long coughing fit on the roof of the house opposite and, at that precise moment, four shadows crept alongside the corpse of the naked woman lying on the pavement, hoisted her over their shoulders and disappeared. As this was happening, in a residential hotel, two women, servants of the club, were carefully masturbating two terrified young men at gun-point who were gradually falling in love.

A dark and dreamy man broke the respectful silence in which the drinkers took such delight.

"Whatever form one thinks love might take, I refuse to divorce it from a feeling of panic and sacred horror. When I met Marie, a sixteen-year-old typist, great purple wings beat unceasingly against my ears. There was not a single minute when, despite all the intersections, gleaming new footpaths did not reflect my face to infinity, lyrical and transfigured. One day, I kissed her in the passage while her boss, an ugly, overbearing shopkeeper with a beard, shouted down from the back office where with stubborn vigilance he guarded the secular dust which had been amassed by three filthy generations of money-grabbers. Did the prestige of the poetry by which I lived make me handsome? Not that I have ever thought myself ugly, but the tender, shy, fair-haired Marie accepted my kisses with a blush. And so it went on for the next few weeks. It only took a second and I was on my knees between two piles of ledgers, making passionate, ridiculous, yet moving declarations of love like those made by characters in novels. My soul played no part in these games. I was overtaken by fears of being emotionally hurt even as Marie let herself become intoxicated with the excitement of her first adventure, I listened religiously to the doubting voice within myself which confronted me with metaphysical problems and populated my sleeplessness with terrible thoughts in which sentimentality, my antagonist's principal weapon, had no part. The lawn sloped gently towards a precipice. Every day I said to myself that I would cease to participate in this stupid, pointless routine. Every day those child-like features, that frank face, expressed such disappointment if, as the day went on, I had not made any of the usual professions that — caught between two heavens, her love for me and the somewhat noble possibility of sparing her pain — I would once again fall at her feet. One summer's day, towards noon, as I watched the sun casting its golden light over a government building, kneeling drunkenly at her feet while she dreamed, my hand lifted up her skirt. She was wearing the sort of drawers that only a virtuous young girl would wear. There was a slash in them, and I clearly caught a glimpse of flesh. Her face showed no sign of indignation but simply awe at the working of a miracle. With unexpected firmness she pulled down her skirt so that I could do nothing more than clasp her buttocks through the fabric of her drawers. She quivered and broke away from me.

"I went no further until I left this firm where the snails crawled over the tricoloured paper of double-entry book-keeping.

"I complimented myself on the abrupt nature of this separation which brought a difficult situation to an end. It was not really her in particular that I loved, I loved her in general. I felt great affection for her and the idea of making her suffer caused me inconceivable pain.

"I bumped into her a few months later. I saw her coming towards me long before she noticed me. I contemplated hiding, but a force which was not to be ignored prevented me from doing so. When we were a few metres apart, our looks crossed. Her dreamy, unforgettable face lit up. An angelic surprise, a profound joy, made her skin flush. She came towards me, without uttering a word, and we made our way towards the Seine down a depressing street whose balconies were laden with gilt signs. Coming out not far from Notre-Dame, in the Square de l'Archevêque, we came to a halt. She listened to the inadequate explanation I gave her for my silence and, once again, I obeyed the prayer in her eyes and kissed her.

"I saw her a number of times towards one o'clock in the afternoon in these quiet public gardens, without bringing my desire for a definite rupture to a head. I was always drawn to her again. Patiently, come rain or shine, she came every day at the same time to await my return. Which, in fact, was exactly what happened. Lies and deep kisses, I always came back...

"Sometimes, before meeting her, I unbuttoned my trousers under my overcoat. Our kisses caused me an exquisite anguish.

" 'Marie,' I said to her, 'look at me.'

"She did as I asked. The square was deserted.

" 'My overcoat is done up. There is something beneath it. Undo my overcoat.'

" 'No. Why do you want me to?'

" 'And what about if I won't want to see you again?'

"Her eyes filled with tears.

" 'Unbutton me.'

" 'No,' she said, 'please don't make me.'

" 'What are you scared of, girl? It has to happen sooner or later...'

"Still she hesitated, then making up her mind, her eyes glued to the ground, she undid the three buttons.

" 'Look.'

"A puerile smile hovered on her lips. She looked down rapidly.

"I insisted more vehemently, again and again, and each time her blush made her all the more desirable as she furtively glanced down.

"Every day I succumbed to the same temptation. First, I got her to unbutton my flies, then to extricate the throbbing flesh.

"We would meet in the church of Saint-Julien-le-Pauvre,[16] under the pretext of visiting Dante's Pastures and there, in front of the statue of M. de Montyon,[17] she would kiss me on the mouth and hold my sex in her tiny hand. I would masturbate in front of her; or I would force her to perform this frenzied activity for me. I found her large eyes, blonde hair and childish clothes strangely exciting. She carried out my orders despite herself, sadly, though she was eager to please me. I made her touch all the most intimate parts of my body. I never managed to place my lips higher than the band of flesh separating her garters and her drawers, drawers, as I have already said, such as a young girl would wear, embroidered, trimmed and hemmed by a maladroit hand.

"Finally, after she had literally possessed me, without allowing me any favours in return (I could have persuaded her to consummate our relationship on a bed of anguish), I wrenched myself away from these wearisome meetings. She telephoned me a number of times at the office, where my work was once again claiming my undivided attention. I got a friend to tell her that I had gone off to some remote country, the first one which sprang to mind: Poland.

"I could hear her voice, disappointed and upset, coming from the receiver.

"She still visits me occasionally, amidst a welter of memories, just before I fall asleep."

Those present started to become garrulous. Another recounted this story.

"Wonderful Lucie! She was a model in a funeral parlour. All day long she tried on black dresses for the benefit of tearful widows, dry-eyed mothers and orphans still in a state of shock. In a black crêpe wimple or a loose blouse of almost flirtatious design, her palpitating and milky breasts aroused the desire of the world-weary lover who asks of love only that it should be an opium beyond the reach of the courts. Ceremonious veils enveloped her, casting curiously erotic grids across the deathly pallor of her skin. Sometimes she wore austere dresses with a high collar, long sleeves and a veil pulled down over her face; sometimes bodices with a deep cleavage, which bared the base of her neck and exaggerated her breasts, with short or transparent sleeves, and silk stockings. The mere sight of this seductive apparition caused some women to renounce living in the past and long instead for a more dramatic existence, in some remote place, shrouded in fog and burning with the bloody kisses of some long-standing and obsessive passion. Little girls would call her mama, implying by this word a tenderness which was anything but filial. Outside the fashion house which employed her, Lucie always dressed in blue. She was as obstinate about wearing this colour as destiny was about making her wear black.

"I saw her through the bay window of the shop where she worked near the Madeleine. A rendezvous traced with a finger in the condensation on the window pane left me in a state of excitement which lasted until evening. How great was my stupefaction when an immense pale blue butterfly approached me. The dust from its wings remained in the lining of my clothes for a long time afterwards.

"That is the whole story of Lucie, together with a clipping from a newspaper detailing the discovery of the decapitated body of a naked woman in a torrent in the Auvergne."

The main room of the club was pervaded by innumerable patches of light and shadow. Shadows of armchairs, shadows of drinkers, shadows of window frames looking out on to the sky, and in each of these shadows the drinkers lodged their dearest love, wings still beating, still trembling with the riotous blood in which they had been steeped until the evening on which they had liberated themselves, to come and briefly take refuge among the butterflies of the night.

One after the other, the drinkers told their stories:

"Roger's eye, Roger's mouth, his hands, especially his hands, Roger's hands, pale and slender, tonight I clutch at these fragments of the person I adored as on other nights I foresee my own death so exactly that it makes my mouth water and blurs my eyes without tears.

"I can still see Roger just as he appeared to my puffy eyes in the morning, when the day rubbed its harsh sleeves across our foreheads, shedding light on the bed where we lay together. His steely muscles and his unblemished forehead, the regularity of his breathing, the powerful yet delicate movement of his chest, everything conspired to bestow on him the masculine physique of the perfect man. As for myself, even if I have aged, I still had plenty of vigour about me, and you may easily believe me when I tell you that by my strength, agility and size, without an ounce of fat, though by no means wiry, I was a splendid specimen of the race. It was two men who wrestled there at night without respite, each ceding to the other in turn. Our pederasty had nothing hybrid about it and we both felt nothing but contempt, a contempt born of ignorance, for men who thought they should have been born women. We avoided them on our path, these female hearts, brains like filter-paper. We kept well away from their gardens, planted with irises, and all the puerile sentimentality and silliness which is as peculiar to them as cheap perfume to a common maid. Their incommensurable foolishness made us smile, and if we defended their behaviour, as generally we did, in the name of individual liberty and the principle that everything is permitted in love as opposed to the proverbial good sense of the normal masses, we also fought against the way some of them cut themselves off from women, either because of impotency or weak constitutions, or out of stupidity, or in the name of the same principle. Roger and I became drunk on our embraces as a result of a quarrel that ended up in a fight, embraces which became amorous when, having been forced to admit that neither of us was capable of overpowering the other, and reconciled through this knowledge, we recognised that our equally antagonistic spirits were on the same level and could confront each other without loss of face.

"Our relationship lasted several years, during which time our hearts and souls fought like precious swords, becoming more finely honed by the day.

"Our love had nothing platonic about it. My arms remember the exact shape of his hips and my lips are capable of matching the shape of his lips. As for him, had he not died, his memories would have been as sharp as mine. The love that I have since unquestionably felt or endured for women, some of whom were admirable creatures, was of an altogether different kind. The desire to vanquish, the nihilism always implicit in love, varies according to the weapons which are employed. Roger and I employed the same weapons, but with women it doesn't happen like that, it being a question for them of overcoming a different nature. For years Roger and I had the sensation of confronting our own reflections in an ideal mirror, for all our gestures, all our thoughts were annihilated by a movement, an identical and inevitable thought.

"Then destiny, in the form of some common illness or other, carried him off, as they say, and I never heard of him again."

During this time, the mermaid with the new scales was asleep in the concierge's lodge full of the Henri II furniture.

Have you ever met a mermaid?

I am sorry for you if you haven't. For my part, there is not a morning when one of them fails to come to my bedside, still wet from the waves of darkness. This mermaid, however, was asleep on my bed. From time to time, when a bell rang, she pulled the cord. The sound of footsteps, sometimes fast, sometimes slow, indicated someone was going past on the staircase, followed by the noise, generator of dreams, of the lift and the closing of a door.

The landscape in which our heroes move is composed, let us not forget, of a modern house on the ground floor of which a white mermaid is preparing herself for bloody adventures, while on the third floor adventurous men are willing to risk sensational perils for the sake of love.

On the pavement opposite this house, a large pool of blood with footprints going away from it; on top of the house, Bébé Cadum; over all this, the memory of Louise Lame. The latter, led on by chance in asbestos gloves, turns into the street which slowly prepares itself for the coming drama. At this very moment the mermaid goes out, and a fight immediately starts between these two creatures.

The absence of water is undoubtedly a disadvantage to the mythological deserter, but the night and the surprise which paralyses Louise Lame evens up the combat.

The two of them roll about the pavement accompanied by the metallic sound of scales being torn off and the soft sound of flesh striking the paving-stones. The street-lamps conventionally illuminate the struggle which is now under way in a pool of blood.

At the club window, Corsair Sanglot pressed his feverish forehead against the coolness of the glass. He gazed at the amazing spectacle for a moment while a rather young man recounted his story.

"Ineffable mark of love! You bestow a new perfume on men's bodies, absolutely different from that of virginity, you provide our minds with a new source of anxiety when we realise that the unknown is even more unrecognisable after the first encounter than when we were ridiculously free of any wound. I was Mabel's lover for no more than a couple of days, but it was enough to change my life and to endow my dreams with a new sense, that of smell. Nights of blood, nights of dreams, nights of love, you now are my nights. As soon as the sun disappears beneath the horizon like the balance-weight of a clock, I feel the tyrannical presence of the stoppered bottles take their customary place after a few light bumps on the shelves of my thoughts. I do not know the names of their ingredients, with one exception, ambergris, which has already bewitched the author of these lines, but at the mere sight of the quivering of this liquid generative of the infinite, my eyes, despite their natural humidity and their natural resemblance, like all eyes, to precious phials, my eyes become more fixed than the geometric points in space where the planets make rendezvous with each other.

"Widen, eyes! It was a July evening, heavy with storm. Mabel, naked, had thrown across her shoulders a multicoloured, transparent shawl which did not even reach down to her stomach. We watched through the open window the far-off clouds swell behind the ring of gasometers and threaten the hot and breathless town. The smell of the pavements rose up dizzily, and love's desires became heavier and more gloomy. Mabel and I, intertwined, without a word, looked at each other.

"I stood up. I grabbed a large bottle of ambergris from a cupboard and began, drop by drop, to spread its contents over this woman's body. The drops fell in turn on the points of her breasts, her navel, each finger, her neck, her most intimate parts. Then, knowing that she would die of this voluptuousness which caused her to writhe on the divan, I was seized with frenzy. Drops fell on her eyes, nostrils, mouth. Soon, her entire body was moistened.

"The only sign of life she showed was a spasmodic breathing. I realised that the bottle was empty. The smell of ambergris filled the room. I was drunk on dream. I broke the neck of the bottle and thrust the jagged edges in turn into her eyes, then her lips, stomach and breasts.

"Then I left, completely impregnated with the triple perfume of blood, love and ambergris.

"I closed the door behind me.

"From time to time, I walk past in the street. I look up at the open window where the curtain still trembles. I think of Mabel with her blood-clotted eyes. And I go away again."

At this moment the mermaid gets to her feet. The body of Louise Lame, vanquished and weary, lies in the pool of blood. The attentive Corsair understands that the time has arrived for reprisals. He was getting ready to go out when the mermaid reappears in the room. He seizes her round the waist, picks her up and sends her sailing through a window into the street. The window panes shatter and water floods into the club: a frothing, blue water, which overturns the tables, the armchairs, the drinkers. Meanwhile, Corsair Sanglot moves away from a district which is so peaceful that dreams become reality there. His path is that of thought, bracken with its peacock's tail. In this way he reaches the foot of the gas-works. The gasometers are filled with the hum of many thousands of butterflies which while away the time, before the moment they are consumed, by beating their wings. The sky of ink and blotting-paper weighs heavily over this tableau.

Corsair Sanglot, your wait would have been long were it not for the invincible destiny which delivers you into my hands.

And now here comes the sponge-seller.

Corsair Sanglot gives him an enquiring look and he reveals that his poetic burden does not suggest to him ideas which are normal.

These are not underwater landscapes stained with the blood of corals, the combats of voracious fish, the wounds of the shipwrecked whose blood rises nebulously to the surface. The next day, passing in this vicinity on a steam-boat, the beautiful millionairess who will, at a later date, be saved from sun-stroke by a miraculous parasol after a celebrated shipwreck, expressed the desire to swim in the transparent, coloured water. The engines were stopped. The roar of the turbines ceased. The quick commands of the black-gloved officers rang out for a moment, then all was silence. The passengers leant on the rails. The young millionairess dived over the side, wearing only a tiny, thin, white bathing-costume. She swam about for half an hour, surprised to discover that the water did not taste of salt but of phosphor. When she climbs back on the bridge, she will be completely red, red as a magnificent flower, a fact not without relevance to the disaster. The men, who had been madly in love with her ever since they had left some European port, would become frenetic, the last topsman, the ship's captain and the engineers being by no means amongst the least smitten. The boat continued on its briefly interrupted voyage, but all eyes, accustomed until then to taking in the horizontal marriage of sea and sky, henceforth saw dancing before them a tyrannical red spectre. Red as the alarm signals situated alongside railway lines, red as the conflagration of a ship loaded with gunpowder, red as wine. Soon, it mingled with the flames of the fire-boxes of the engines, with the folds of the flags flapping at the tops of the masts towards the stern, with the flight of birds over the open seas and tropical fish. Extraordinarily, phallic icebergs drifted down as far as these warm seas. One night, they arrived at the transversal wake and the spectre was reflected in them better than in a mirror. At this point a savage embrace brought the long cruise to an abrupt halt.

No, these are not the common stories that sponges learn from their seller who walks naked down the street lined with gasometers. Nor are they the stories of those sea-turtle hunters who one day felt the presence of an unaccustomed weight in their net. Hauling it in with difficulty, they discovered in the mesh an ancient mutilated bust and a mermaid: a mermaid who was a fish down to the waist and a woman from the waist to her feet. From that day on, existence became unbearable on board the little boat. The nets no longer contained anything except silky, plump starfish, jelly-fish as flaccid and transparent as recently murdered dancers wearing tutus, anemones and magical algae. The water in the tanks changed into genuine pearls, the provisions into Alpine flowers, edelweiss and clematis. The sailors were racked with hunger without any of them dreaming of throwing back into the sea the augural creature responsible for the famine. She dreamed on the prow, her new existence seeming to cause her no pain. The crew died within a few days and the skiff, plaything of the currents, still wanders the oceans.

No, this story does not slumber in the nights of the sponge-seller, neither this nor that of the phantom vessel whose wake is luminous, nor the treasure of the buccaneers, nor the submerged ruins.

He raises his hand and speaks. He says that, on his back, he carries the thirty sponges soaked in bile which were offered to Christ to appease his thirst. He says that, for nineteen hundred years, these sponges have served to titivate fatally attractive women and that they have the property of rendering their adorable flesh even more diaphanous. He says that these thirty sponges have dried tears of sadness and tears of joy, effaced forever all trace of nights of battle and half-death. He exhibits them one at a time, these sacred sponges which have touched the lips of the satanic masochist. O Christ! Lover of sponges! Corsair Sanglot, the seller, and I alone know of your love for the voluptuous sponges, for the tender, elastic and refreshing sponges whose salty taste is comforting to mouths tortured by bloodthirsty kisses and ringing words.

That is why henceforth you shall partake of the sacrament in the form of the sponge.

The sacred sponge which flattens itself in the hollow between the shoulder blades and against the nascent breasts, on the neck and on the waist, at the birth of the loins and on the triangle of the thighs, which disappears between muscular buttocks and the dark corridor of passion, which is crushed and sobs beneath the naked feet of women.

We shall partake of the sacrament in the form of the sponge, we shall press it against our eyes which have stared too long at the inside wall of the lid, which know too well the mechanics of tears to wish to make use of them. We shall press it against our symmetrical ears, O Christ, under our tired armpits.

The sponge-seller passes in the streets. How late it is. The sandman had preceded him and had scattered sterile beaches here and there. Here is the sponge-seller who throws love at tormented lovers (as if those who are not breathless with anxiety merit the name of lovers).

The sponge-seller has passed. Here is the mattress and here is the pillow, both are soft. Let us go to sleep.

The sponge-seller is now far away from the haloed gasometers.

Corsair Sanglot reflected. He remembered a woman's body and a room where one drank a sweet liquid... He makes his way back to the Sperm Drinkers' Club.

He finds the street again.

He does not find the corpse.

He finds the remains of the white mermaid, half-skeleton and half-fishbone. He finds his armchair and his cup. He finds the drinkers, his companions. He rediscovers, on top of the house opposite, the ever-present Bébé Cadum.

A drinker begins to speak as he enters.

"When midnight strikes, it will be exactly twenty-three years since my bedroom door opened and the wind first ushered in an immense head of blonde hair then…"

VIII. *As Far as the Eye Can See*

Corsair Sanglot was bored! Boredom had become his main reason to go on living. He let it grow in silence, marvelling every day that it still managed to increase in size. It was Boredom: a large sunny square, lined with rectilinear colonnades, perfectly swept, perfectly clean, deserted. An unalterable hour had struck in the Corsair's life and he now understood that boredom is synonymous with Eternity. In vain was he awakened every night by the pendulum's strange tick-tock, a tick-tock which grew ever louder, filling the room in which he lay with the sound of its breathing or else, towards midnight, a dark presence which would interrupt his dream. His pupils, dilated in the darkness, sought for the person who must have come into the room. But no one had forced the door and soon the calm sound of the clock mingled with the sleeper's breathing.

Corsair Sanglot felt a new sense of self-esteem growing within himself. Since he had understood and accepted the monotony of Eternity, he advanced straight as a pole through adventures, slithering vines which were unable to check his progress. A new exaltation had replaced his depression. A sort of enthusiasm in reverse permitted him to consider objectively the failure of his most cherished enterprises. Time's freedom had finally conquered him. He had merged with the patient minutes which succeeded and resembled one another.

It was boredom, the great square into which he had one day ventured. It was three o'clock in the afternoon. Silence weighed over everything, even the sonorous buzzing of hornets and the heated air. The colonnades cast their rectilinear shadows over the yellow ground. No passers-by, except on the other side of the square, which must have had a three-kilometre radius: a tiny person strolling without visible purpose. Corsair Sanglot remarked with terror that it was still three o'clock, that the shadows were immutably turned in the same direction. But this terror was dispelled. The Corsair finally came to terms with this pathetic hell. He knew that no paradise was permitted to the man who suddenly became aware one day of the existence of the infinite, and he agreed to remain, an eternal sentinel, on the square that was warmed and brilliantly lit by an immobile sun.

Who was it who compared boredom to dust? Boredom and eternity are absolutely devoid of the least speck of dust. A mental road-sweeper carefully attends to the hopeless cleanliness. Did I say hopeless? Boredom may no more engender hopelessness than it may culminate in suicide. You who have no fear of death, try a little boredom. Henceforth, death will no longer be of the slightest use to you. The immobile torment and the distant perspectives of the mind freed of all sense of the picturesque and all sentimentality will have been revealed to you once and for all.

It was at this period of his life that a strange adventure happened to Corsair Sanglot. Not that he got too excited about it.

He scarcely deigned to pay the slightest attention to the romantic landscape in which his body was moving: a sunken road followed the wall of a cemetery behind which could be seen the tops of some cypress trees and two gigantic parasol pines while the sky became convulsed, swollen with grey and black clouds, clouds rent asunder to the west by a fan of sunbeams which only made the monstrous vaults of the heavy cumulus stand out all the more lugubriously. Three o'clock was it? It was more like five o'clock on a September evening. The desolation of dusk's dark cloak advanced across the land. The only noise audible was the unlikely clatter of a car engine, presumably on a concealed road cut into a nearby embankment, unless the lowness of the clouds caused the sound to travel further than usual.

Suddenly, and Corsair Sanglot did not see this, thirty thousand tombstones in the cemetery rose up and thirty thousand cadavers in calico night-shirts appeared lined up as if on parade. A couple of them broke away and, scaling the stones, leaned their elbows on the ridge of the wall. It was at this moment that Corsair Sanglot, who was feeling slightly depressed, noticed their heads. They projected unexpectedly above the level of the wall and stared at him laughingly, but as for him, he just continued on his way. Their peals of laughter echoed long behind him, and the sound of the invisible car engine suddenly became much louder. When the Corsair arrived at the place where the path joined the road, he saw an enormous hearse, a giant's hearse, pulled by four strong Percherons whose hoofs, partly hidden by a fringe of hair, drummed heavily against the ground, though the hearse was empty, with neither a coffin nor a coachman.

It disappeared. The corpses on the cemetery wall studied the sky in silence. The sky, where one would have preferred the brightness of a storm, buffeted by currents of air high above, became convulsed with great banks of grey and black clouds which totally altered the colour of the dying day and gave to nature a bituminous aspect, heavy and lowering. The stormy boredom of the high seasons enveloped Corsair Sanglot in its gloomy sponge-cloth dressing-gown. It is he who, with a vigilant finger, moved the illusory hands of the clock face. It is he who confused the passers-by on the large sunny squares lined with colonnades, and it is he who, with a steady hand, agitated his slack ocean, ignoring tempests despite a sky full of menacing grey and black clouds too oily in which to drown oneself.

Various landscapes in keeping with the casting of spells: from the cave in which the Sibyl and her serpentine familiar presided over the fall of Empires to the tunnels of the Metro decorated with their monotonously humorous posters for Dubonnet, ridiculous name, destined to exorcise the ghostly familiars of underground passageways, by way of the Bondy forests, blooming with blunderbusses and musketoons, populated by bandits in conical hats, granite-built feudal manor houses with vaulted chambers haunted by friendly ravens and voluminous owls; to the flats of the petit-bourgeoisie where, as a result of some insignificant pretext, an upset salt-cellar or a hint of criticism, disagreement with its gun-cotton pyroxylin breasts enters without knocking and runs up to the soft-spoken parents and their pusillanimous son, placing in their hand the until that moment inoffensive bread-knife (except for fingers cut when slicing bread — one should break bread, not cut it, do this in remembrance of our Lord) or while chopping parsley (a dangerous herb because of its resemblance to hemlock, a poisonous plant of which Socrates was sentenced to swallow a fatal dose by the merciless tribunal of an ungrateful country, which enabled the hero dear to pederasts to display tremendous courage in the face of death and so aggrandise himself at the very moment his enemies hoped to see him off) in order to transform the peaceful dining-room into a frightful slaughterhouse, blood spurting from severed carotids, spattering one after the other the soup tureen of Limoges china, the gas chandelier and the imitation Renaissance buffet; to the street corners lit by green lamps to indicate bus stops, at which gallows-bird shadows hold secret confabulations, huddled in the shadows of entrances, until the very moment when they are alerted by echoing footsteps that the time is ripe for them to jump out on unsuspecting pedestrians; to the ripe meadows at two o'clock in the afternoon when the tourist, at a loss as to what to do, unbuttons his flies and falls on his knees astride the young shepherdess with her skirts bundled up above her waist. Landscapes: you are only cardboard stage-sets. A single actor: Frégoli,[18] that is to say boredom, struts about the stage and plays out a sempiternal farce in which the protagonists pursue each other never-endingly, forever obliged to change costumes in the wings before each new reincarnation.

Not long afterwards, Corsair Sanglot went down a Parisian street.

MONOLOGUE OF CORSAIR SANGLOT OUTSIDE
A BARBER'S SHOP ON THE RUE DU FAUBOURG-SAINT-HONORÉ

"I have never had any friends, only lovers. Given the strength of attachment I felt for my friends and my coldness towards women, for a long time I used to think that I was more capable of friendship than love. Sheer madness, I was totally incapable of friendship. The passionate nature of my relations with all sorts of people, how could I discard it or transfer it to other recipients. In some cases, I remember, the passion was reciprocal. Those tumultuous encounters, that furious attraction, that half-hatred, those crises of conscience, the rows, the sense of sadness when they were not there, the different emotions with which, now we hardly ever see each other any more, I think of them — how could I possibly mistake those things for that grey and shapeless entity called friendship. Those incapable of sensing the exalted character of the exchange I was offering gave me friendship, and I despised them. Friends became part of my life for no more than a moment. We abandoned each other, not without jealousy, for the first pretty face. I lost myself in alcoves without echoes, they too. I believed in the profound oblivion of sleeping with your head on your mistress's breast, I let myself be taken in by the tenderness of the female sphinx, they too. Nothing can bring back for us the way we were. Strangers to each other when together, the communion of ideas we once enjoyed revives only when we have gone our separate ways. Our memories are not the slightest help. Confronted by one of our former friends, that idealised friend — the one we imagine we are with when we are alone — asks with whom we are comparing him and what right we have to behave in such a way, he who is but a fiction, the product of the melancholic notion of the void.

"And now I have no other setting for my actions than the public squares: Place La Fayette, Place des Victoires, Place Vendôme, Place Dauphine, Place de la Concorde.

"A poetic agoraphobia transforms my nights into deserts and my dreams into anxieties.

"I am speaking today from outside a window of periwigs and tortoise-shell combs and as I automatically stock this greenhouse with severed heads and apathetic turtles, a gigantic razor made of the finest steel takes the place of the hand on the clock face of my tiny imagination. From now on, it will shave the minutes without cutting them off.

"My former mistresses change their hair-styles and I no longer see them; somewhere or other, with a growing affection, my friends drink ominous aperitifs with strangers.

"I am alone: still capable, more than capable, of feeling passion. Boredom, the boredom which I cultivate with a rigorous lack of awareness, guards my life from the uniformity whence spring storms and night and the sun."

At this moment the barber came out to stand in the shop doorway and examine the stationary passer-by.

"Would you care for a shave, sir, I won't hurt you. My nickel-plated instruments are nimble elves. My wife, the wig-maker with hair the colour of Brazilian rosewood, is renowned for the adroitness of her massage and the dexterity of her manicure. Step this way, sir; come on in."

The barber's chair and the mirror extended their usual gloom. The shaving-dish was already brimming with lather. The barber prepared the shaving-brush. It was two o'clock in the morning, night jumbled up the shadows cast by the waxwork busts. A smell of cologne hung heavily in the air. The lather on the shaving-sticks made a crackling sound as it dried. Corsair Sanglot felt a strange presence above his head. He ripped away the sheet violently and the salty air of the expiring sea at his feet made him feel light-headed. The sand was smooth.

Next Corsair Sanglot got lost in an enormous palace dotted with high columns, columns so high that the ceiling was invisible. Then his historiographer lost him from sight and forgot about him.

The Corsair went on walking. The palace kept him occupied for a long time. Constructed from the shells of lobsters and crayfish, and set in the midst of white mountains, its slender shape and the red mass of its towers reached upwards. In the sides of the walls of those towers, which were made from the shells of turtle crabs, care had been taken to use shellfish, cooked and brown, while the sea breeze caused the entire edifice to rock gently on its fragile foundations.

Do not become my friend, I warn you. I have sworn never to let myself be taken in by that terrible MAN-TRAP. I will never be your friend and if you agree to give up everything for me, I will still abandon you one day.

In any case, I know the feeling of being abandoned only too well, having experienced it myself. If that is the insolent luxury you desire, that is fine; you may follow me. Otherwise all I ask of you is your indifference, if not your enmity.

IX. *The Palace of Mirages*

Lost in the desert, the white-helmeted explorer sees the majestic towers of an unknown city looming on the horizon.

Corsair Sanglot was walking through the gardens of the Tuileries at three o'clock in the afternoon on his way towards the Concorde. At the same moment Louise Lame was going down the Rue Royale. As she passes Maxim's café, the wind lifts her hat and whisks it away in the direction of the Madeleine. Louise Lame, dishevelled, chases after it and picks it up. While this is happening, Corsair Sanglot crosses the Place de la Concorde and disappears down the Avenue Gabrielle. Three minutes later, Louise Lame in turn crosses the square, once illustrious for its revolutionary machinery, and begins to make her way along the Avenue des Champs-Élysées. Corsair Sanglot pauses for a second to do up his shoe-laces. He lights a cigarette. Louise Lame and Corsair Sanglot, separated by the clumps of trees along the Champs-Élysées, move in parallel in the same direction.

Lost in the desert, the white-helmeted explorer consults the position of the night stars in vain. On the horizon loom the formidable machicolated towers of an unknown city whose shadow covers a vast territory. Corsair Sanglot remembers a woman he once met long ago on the Rue du Mont-Thabor. Jack the Ripper's very own bedroom provided shelter for them. He is surprised that his thoughts cling to her so insistently, he wishes ardently to meet this woman again. And Louise Lame, bothered by the exactness of her memories, wonders what ever became of that handsome buccaneer who surrendered himself to her one evening. On the blackboard in a ruinous secondary-school lecture hall, a school lost in the suburbs of a populous city and the lair of lost cats, circumstance's black genius traces itineraries which cross but do not meet. Lost in a desert without palm trees, the white-helmeted explorer slowly circles a mysterious city unknown to geographers.

Corsair Sanglot turns right. Louise Lame left. The white-helmeted explorer approaches nearer and nearer the city sprung up in the middle of the desert. It shrinks soon to a tiny sandcastle which is dispersed by the wind, while misgivings assail the lonely traveller who can only wonder what new power has been bestowed on his glance.

The genius of circumstance puts on his road-mender's uniform, makes his way to the Place de la Concorde and there traces mysterious stars on the pavement.

Louise Lame, proceeding on her way, suddenly sees the Corsair standing in her path. But it was only a dream. For a long time she contemplates the place where his ghost appeared. She is thinking to herself that one day, not so long ago perhaps, the adventurer himself had undoubtedly set foot in the same place where she now stood. She started out again pensively.

As for him, the wind inflating the pleats of his raglan overcoat, his reflection in the windows and mirrors ahead, following the direction of his fleeting thoughts, now stained scarlet and then green in front of chemists' shops, now brushed by the fur of a woman's coat, he let himself be borne away towards the Gare Saint-Lazare. From the Boulevard des Batignolles, he looks down into the sooty cutting and sees trains leaving Paris. As it is not yet dark, the street-lamps cast a pale, yellow light across the doors. Against one of them is leaning the mermaid from the Sperm Drinkers' Club. The Corsair does not see her.

Lost in the desert, the white-helmeted explorer discovers the real remains, buried in the sand until uncovered by a recent sirocco, of a former Timbuktu. Going down the stairs from the flat where he has just committed his latest masterpiece, Jack the Ripper strolls down the Boulevard des Batignolles. He begs a light from the Corsair for his cigarette which has gone out, and a few metres further on asks a policeman the shortest route to Ternes. Lost in a desert of black sand, the white-helmeted explorer enters the ruins of the former Timbuktu. He is greeted by the sight of treasure and skeletons bearing the esoteric symbols of a long dead religion. The express train in which the mermaid has taken a seat crosses a bridge at the very same moment the German music-hall chanteuse drives over it in a car. Corsair Sanglot, Louise Lame and the chanteuse's desire for each other spreads in vain across the entire world. Their thoughts jostle each other, increasing their desire to meet as they collide at those mysterious points of infinity where they are reflected back towards the minds which have given rise to them. Prostrate yourself before these places of destiny where remarkable people, for whom such meetings are crucial, continually miss each other by a minute. Strange destiny by which Corsair Sanglot and Louise Lame almost brush against each other on the Place de la Concorde, by which the mermaid and the chanteuse pass, one beneath the other in a sinister corner of a Parisian suburb, by which you or I, in a bus or any other means of public transport, take a seat in front of the very person who is able to unite us with the man or woman who has been lost in our memories since the time of our nights of torment, without us knowing it, strange destiny how long will you frustrate our tired and troubled senses?

Lost in a desert of coal and anthracite, an explorer dressed in white recalls the evening fire in the rustic grate at his parents-in-law's, when his wife was no more than his fiancée; when will-o'-the-wisps were not called St Elmo's fire and, like garden flowers, half seen in the darkness of your eyelids when you clench your eyes shut, they hovered in the marshy countryside; when, the embers dying about one o'clock in the morning of a 25 December, a young child wakes and, wearing only a night-shirt, goes to check that the mythological hero has passed through the paternal hearth, and listens to the roar of the wind in the chimney which accompanies the song of invisible archangels who inculcate in him a love of the night and a love of the midday sun, as unvarying, solemn and tragic as the shadows; when the aurora borealis was glimpsed for the first time rising in the north in the magical drawings of a book for children, before being rapturously greeted on the bridge of a boat in a forgotten bay in the Arctic circle.

A cobblestone from the Place de la Concorde, left over by some workmen, dislodges itself from the pile where it has until then been condemned by its mineralogical properties. It addresses the people there, speaking their language which, despite being an unusual phenomenon, would hardly have retained their interest (given that the crowd are accustomed to prodigies) if it had not also enumerated the names of all those who had trodden on it over the course of the years. The names of the famous are greeted with cheers and shouts. There then follow unfamiliar names, the names of humble individuals, repeated far and wide by loud-speakers, names which echo ponderously in the hearts of all those gathered there. Someone recognises the name of his father, another person, an old man, raises his hat upon hearing the name of his first mistress, others recognise their own surnames. They come to a halt and their lives seem pitiful to them. Boredom invaded each one's mind. Corsair Sanglot takes note of the depressed state of public opinion. He rejoices and is amazed at his strange joy. He understands at last that in place of boredom he has discovered a despair identical with enthusiasm.

Lost between segments of a ferocious horizon, the white-helmeted explorer prepares to die and assembles his memories in order to discover how an explorer should end his days: with his arms outstretched and his face in the sand, or should he dig a fugitive tomb because of wind and hyenas, or just curl up in the so-called broken-gun position which causes so much worry to mothers when they discover that this is the position in which their offspring prefer to fall asleep, or will it be a lion or sunstroke or thirst that does the honours for him.

The cobblestone in the Place de la Concorde considers the procession of all those who have stepped on it. Women's underclothing, varying according to fashion, adventurers, those out for a peaceful stroll, women's underclothing, horsemen, coaches, barouches, victorias, cabriolets, hackney carriages, cars, Corsair Sanglot, Louise Lame, So-and-so, cars, policemen, you, me, Corsair

Sanglot, cars, cars, cars, night prowlers, policemen, lamp-lighters, Corsair Sanglot, someone else, someone else.

Two Metro lines, two trains, two carriages, two people walking in parallel streets, two lives, couples criss-crossing without seeing each other, potential encounters, meetings which shall never take place. The imagination rewrites history. It modifies the local directory and the roll-call of those who frequent a town, a street, a house, a woman. It transfixes reflections in the mirror for all eternity. It hangs entire portrait galleries from the wall of our future memory on which magnificent strangers use a sharp knife to engrave their initials and a date.

Corsair Sanglot, on the third floor of a house, is still thinking of the legendary Louise Lame while the latter, on the third floor of another house, remembers him as he was the evening they parted, and through the walls their eyes meet and, to the amazement of astronomers, give birth to new stars. Face to face, but hidden by how many obstacles, houses, public monuments, trees, the two converse inwardly with each other.

Let a tumultuous catastrophe topple the screens and the circumstances and there they are, grains of sand lost on a flat plain, united by the imaginary straight line which links every being to no matter what other being. Neither time nor space, nothing opposes these ideal relations. A life overturned, worldly constraints, earthly obligations, everything crumbles. Human beings are no less subject to the same arbitrary roll of the dice.

In the desert, lost, irremediably lost, the white-helmeted explorer finally realises the reality of mirages and of unknown treasures, the dream-like fauna, the improbable flora which constitute the sensual paradise where from now on he will evolve, a scarecrow without sparrows, a tomb without epitaph, a man without name, while, in a formidable displacement, the pyramids reveal the dice hidden beneath their heavy mass and pose once more the perplexing problem of bygone fatality and future destiny. As for the present, that beautiful eternal sky, it lasts no longer than the time it takes to roll three dice over a city, a desert, a man, a white-helmeted explorer, more lost in his vast intuition of eternal events than in the sandy expanse of the equatorial plain where his genius, that wily guide, has led him step by step towards a revelation which ceaselessly contradicts itself and causes him to stray from his own unrecognisable image, due to the position of his eyes or the lack of some point of comparison and the legitimate suspicions which a superior spirit always entertains for mirrors whose revealed truth remains wholly uncorroborated, leading him to the chaotic image of the skies, other beings, inanimate objects and the ghostly incarnations of his own thoughts.

The Boarding-School at Humming-Bird Garden

he calm, well-raked gardens before the imposing house offered their green lawns and geometric avenues to the games of little girls. When I say offered, I ought to have added during the day. It was night-time now. The imposing building rose up, pierced in three places by lighted windows against the perfectly blue backdrop of night. On the horizon there are forests stirred by the rustling wind, forests echoing with the screams of owls, the moaning of murdered rabbits (their fur and bones are to be found in piles on the ground, beneath the nests of nocturnal predators), the muffled subterranean labours of moles; there are oceans furrowed by sharks and steamboats, criss-crossed, not far from the coasts, by the comings and goings of destroyers displaying the Union Jack, disturbed by waves, the flicks of porpoises' tails and the thud of wreckage on the reefs, brightened by balls where shrimps and sea-horses dance, glittering with the emigration of sardines and eels, swarming in the shadows of the rocks with crabs and lobsters; there are marshes which act as receivers of bodies, the bodies of those trapped and mummified in horrible postures, the bodies of people who have been murdered by robbers and thrown there after their pockets and luggage have been ransacked; there are white roads and gleaming railway lines, there are the celestial lights of a great city: without doubt London, actually visible or imaginable, as seen from the English county of Kent.

It was eleven o'clock at night. A man, rather young, was awkwardly making his way through the roots and ferns of the forest towards this red-brick building surrounded by flat lawns.

Clouds slowly rose from behind the marsh and filled the sky. Clouds heavy with thunder yet to come and receivers of lightning. The shouts of the hauliers could be heard coming from the direction of the sea.

From one of the windows of the building a sharp sound could be heard. The sound of hard slaps, the crack of a whip. A cry went up, then several more which soon merged into a monotonous moan.

In a classroom, an extremely beautiful thirty-five-year-old woman, her brown hair tinged with red, was spanking a sixteen-year-old girl who was lying across her knees. She began with her hand. The red mark left by her five fingers could still be seen on the delicate flesh. The girl's drawers had been pulled down, imprisoning her knees in lace, and her loose hair hid her face. Her quivering rump spasmodically contracted. The marks slowly disappeared, replaced by the red stripes made by the strict schoolmistress's leather tawse. Sometimes, when a blow particularly hurt, the girl would jerk forwards more than usual, her thighs would open and this sensual sight would cause another young girl, standing in a corner awaiting her turn to be punished, to become aroused.

And now as a streak of lightning is about to appear in the sky which I have evoked, despite its blackness, on the white paper, I understand why the tableau has been composed in this manner. The similarity between the streak of lightning and the slap of the tawse on the white bottom of a sixteen-year-old girl at boarding-school is alone sufficient to call forth the storm in the midst of the impassive night which conceals the house.

Boarding-school at Humming-Bird Garden, you have long existed in my imagination, a red-brick house surrounded by calm lawns — with your dormitories where virgins sense the passage of the son of the virgin at midnight, turning over voluptuously in their beds without waking; with your head-mistress's study, an authoritarian woman with an arsenal of whips, rods and crops; with your classrooms where white figures lost in the depths of the blackboard sympathise with the mysterious signs sketched in the sky by the stars — but while you remain motionless in a landscape of the lesson of things, the storm of all eternity rises up behind your slate roof to break forth, with the brilliance of lightning, at the precise instant when the head-mistress's tawse marks the buttocks of a sixteen-year-old girl boarder with a red furrow and painfully illuminates, like a bolt of lightning, the mysterious arcana of my erotic imagination. Have I not written only in order to evoke your resemblance, lightning, whiplash! And must I describe the appearance of this stormy night, the saturnine but beautiful woman with her breasts which evoke jagged rocks on river banks, her deep black eyes, the black curls of her hair and that complexion identical to summer prunes, who, brandishing a cruel whip in her strong arm, who, despite the disorder of her dark dress, a disorder which reveals her adorable breasts and muscular thighs, goes about her business with a majestic air which fills us with respect.

In the well-lit study of the head-mistress, the punishment comes to an end. The girl, red in the face, hardly makes a whimper. The disciplinarian gives her two or three more strokes of the whip, a few more smacks, then carefully lowers her fine blouse, pulls up her drawers, helps the victim to her feet and points to the corner in which she is to kneel down.

Meanwhile, the man was still walking through the forest. The first drops of rain did not immediately penetrate the thick foliage. There was a smell of damp dust, then that of the leaves, and then that of grass. Finally, rain began to fall on the walker. The path became more difficult. Slipping on the clay, sinking into muddy potholes and piles of leaf-mould hidden by the grass, his face streaming with water from the blows of the lower branches, he made his way towards the clearing. At last, he reached it.

The plain, falling away in a gentle slope, presented a stormy panorama. Bolts of lightning lit up the flaccid underbelly of the clouds, the breaking crests of the forests, or the front of a house which it rendered as white and frightening as a haunted house. The thunder added its occasional rumblings to the unchanging sound of the sea. The wind dropped. The heavy rain of the storm was replaced by a fine drizzle which, because of its monotony, gave an impression of permanence.

The man made for the only house in which a light still shone: the boarding-school of Humming-Bird Garden.

The head-mistress had called over to her the second girl, a sturdy blonde, with two dimples on her cheeks, dimples identical to those which were to be found on her arched white bottom when she too, in turn, found herself flat on her stomach across the knees of her tormentor, trussed up and half-naked.

The relentless disciplinarian paused to contemplate this disturbing vision for a moment, this white flesh which she would soon cover in stripes and which was strangely lost amidst the layers of skirts and petticoats and her rolled-up chemise. She unhooked her suspenders and rolled the stockings down as far as her knees: one leg had come out of her drawers which were hooked around the other foot.

Then, starting just above the knees and working up the body, the adroit tormentor began to slap the fleshy thighs. On the way she paid particular attention to the two superb orbs of the buttocks, white mounds to begin with, then pink turning red, then an almost bloody orange. They tensed under the blows, causing the parting in the middle to diminish until it was a shallow groove. Soon, the muscular mass began to tremble convulsively, contracting and relaxing without control, allowing the brown crack to open in which a plump mouth could be glimpsed, crumpled up and protected by hair. From time to time, as with her companion, a tremendous jerk caused her to bend ever further forward, parting her thighs so that the sex itself was revealed. When the blood was freely flowing beneath the flesh, the head-mistress seized the tawse which left further bloody stripes on the victim's delicate skin. It was the turn of the whip next, then the riding-crop.

The man approached the house. For a moment his imagination was as one with the supernaturally white buildings at the onset of the storm. Meanwhile, the sound of fleshy thwacks attracted his attention. He reached the side of the building and, by means of a waste-water pipe which served the gutters, climbed up as far as the open window from which the sound came.

The punishment was nearly over. The work was now being finished off by hand. Hands which rained down short, sharp blows on the few places which the leather had spared.

When the child was dressed and upright again, the head-mistress stood up and ordered:

"Nancy, you and Dolly undress me ready for bed."

Dolly and Nancy kneeled on the floor. They unlaced her yellow leather shoes and, slipping their tiny hands under her petticoats, they unfastened her suspenders and rolled down her stockings. Standing again, they carefully unhooked her skirt and bodice. The woman appeared dressed in lace cami-knickers and brassière. These two garments were removed in turn. Naked, with firm breasts and gently curved buttocks, the woman completely dominated the two little girls who, following the accustomed ritual, kissed her wicked mouth, her round stomach, her sturdy rump before attiring her in a thin, short night-dress and braiding her luxuriant hair.

It was at that moment that the man clinging to the balcony raised the sash of the window and entered the room. He took from his pocket a black revolver and placed it on the mantelpiece. Picking up the stockings of the woman, who regarded him motionlessly, he imprisoned the head of Dolly in one and the head of Nancy in the other, before finally turning round:

"Show me the way."

She led him down a dark corridor, pushed open a creaking door, and went into a dormitory.

In thirty white beds slept, or rather pretended to sleep, thirty young girls. In the flickering glow of the night-lights, their hair, generally blonde though occasionally red, seemed to shiver. The head-mistress roused the dormitory. Under thirty white sheets, thirty palpitating bodies fidgeted. Their eyes wide open, the children observed this formidable tyrant, Corsair Sanglot, for it is indeed he, somebody new, terrible and delectable as their dreams.

They got up and walked down the varnished pine staircase in procession. The garden smelt just as all the novelists describe it. Imagine, then, thirty young girls, night-dresses rolled up above their waists, kneeling on the green lawn.

And what does the hero of such a thrilling adventure do?

The echoes long reverberated of the punishments inflicted on those excited bodies. The first light of dawn was raising its finger above the forest by the time the Corsair had finished bruising those tender thighs and muscular hips.

After which, he and his terrible mistress, who had witnessed her lover's behaviour without saying a word, embraced each other passionately.

Louise Lame and Corsair Sanglot had again met up with each other. As the Angelus sounded (is the Angelus sounded in England?), they separated. He to return to his path through the dense forest. She to shepherd her pupils, amorous and humiliated, back to their dormitory. She freed Nancy and Dolly who had fallen asleep with a stocking over their heads.

The thirty-two girls slept until midday, awakening with astonishment that they should have been accorded such a privilege. As they watched the bright midday sun shining across their barrow beds, they remembered the events of the night before. Love and jealousy tormented their souls in equal measure. They had to get up and return to their school work. When they had to submit to the head-mistress's whip, a strange emotion would seize hold of them. The memory of their charming but cruel seducer, the hatred of he who had possessed them. Everything occurred as I have said. Soon, in order to evoke more powerfully the gentle morning on which they had encountered love, they even began to flagellate themselves. They spent their play-times behind the blackthorn bushes. And two by two, they whipped each other, blissfully happy when blood circled their thighs like a thin, hot reptile. Corsair Sanglot continued on his solitary path, while in memory of him, on a calm plain covered in woods in the county of Kent, thirty young girls flagellated themselves day and night, counting the scars in the morning with an indescribable pride.

Every evening, as was her custom, the head-mistress selected two victims and led them to her room. And she beat with anger the thighs which he had made suffer. She, too, would have liked to suffer as they had, and a passionate rage possessed her. Because she alone had been unable to satisfy the Corsair.

Like a barbarian, he had first needed to take possession of her pupils, and nothing would ever be able to console those troubled souls again.

Despite the years passing over the smooth lawns and paths and trees of the nearby forest.

Despite the years passing over those furrowed brows, those eyes amorous of shadows, those enervated bodies.

And, one night, the storm rolling across the plain and swamps once again lit up the severe frontage of the house and the marshes full of will-o'-the-wisps.

But Corsair Sanglot never appeared again at the boarding-school where those un-flinchingly faithful hearts await him still, hearts now senile in the foul bodies of old women.

XI. *Roll, Drums of Santerre*

21 January was drawing to a close. Louis XVI mounted the steps to the guillotine.

At the moment Corsair Sanglot emerged from the Rue Royale into the Place de la Concorde — noting with approval that the magnificent obelisk had been replaced by an adorable guillotine — a company of drummers with their white leather baldricks was lining up in a row against the wall of the terrace of the Tuileries while Jean Santerre, their commander, mounted on a dock-tailed and crop-eared horse endowed with an abundant mane, surveyed the spectacle of the crowd gathered round the engine of retribution watching Louis XVI climb the steps like an automaton and closely observing every gesture of the executioner and his assistants who, by means of a nevertheless simple act, were about to transform 21 January into one of the most memorable days ever, a day which gave rise to so much passion, a day whose anniversary does not so much celebrate its memory as recall to the living that it was then that an event took place which would alter the course of the world, a day on which the curtain has not yet fallen, despite the almanacs and all the unnecessary alterations in the calendar.

A roll of drums informed Corsair Sanglot that the king, having desired to speak, had met with the passionate opposition of a heart equal to submerging his voice under the grave sound of these primitive instruments. Corsair Sanglot knew how to die. He had decided upon the date and the time, when he would be a month short of thirty-nine, a June day at dawn. He did not yet know exactly how he would die. He could make a good guess, however, that it would be as a result of injuries received on the Champs-de-Mars, perhaps even a murder. Under a tin-foil sky against which the Eiffel Tower could hardly be seen, the murderers escape towards the Seine and the memory of a woman whom he loved becomes mingled with his sensation of excruciating agony. He is dying, or so it seems to him, amidst a landscape which represents one of the seven wonders of the modern world or else, the following day, in a hard bed, a faint light coming in from the workshop windows above his head, the first workers on their way to the Metro, their feet drumming loudly on the morning pavement. At this moment perhaps, in the Rue Diderot, a convicted murderer, standing between the public prosecutor in a top hat and a bare-headed doctor, would be on the verge of execution. The rustle of the dew-covered trees would constitute, both for him and for the condemned man, the last sign of the material universe. After which, at the very same moment, they, brothers yet total strangers, would fall prey to their dreams. Let none other than him open their mouth at this final moment. It fell to him to order the last roll of the drums and to close upon complete and utter mystery this mouth of tender, cruel and seductive flesh, these eyes more beautiful in death than during love-making. A pine forest springs up in Corsair Sanglot's imagination. Hidden behind its trunks and pine-needles, he observes the mass guillotinings of the Terror. It is a procession of the admired and the despised. The executioner holds up the severed head again and again with exactly the same gesture every time. Ridiculous heads of aristocrats, heads of lovers full of their love, heads of women heroically sentenced to death. But, love and hate, can they inspire other acts? A paper balloon drifts lightly over the theatre of revolution. The Marquis de Sade places his face next to that of Robespierre. Their two profiles stand out against the red lunette of the guillotine and Corsair Sanglot admires this medallion for a moment.

Charenton! Charenton! tranquil suburb troubled only by occasional fights between pimps and solitary drownings, now you lodge the peaceful angler, the kind, almost extinct today, who wears a funnel-shaped straw hat with a little flag on the top. The screams of madmen no longer echo about your disused asylum. His independence of mind will reside there no more, he, the Marquis de Sade, hero of love, of generosity and of liberty, the perfect hero for whom death is truly peaceful. Member of the Section des Piques,[19] we deeply regret the departure of this enlightened and eloquent citizen. The words which he found to extol the memory of the Friend of the People to us still echo in our republican memories. Though born into the ranks of the aristocrats, citizen Sade suffered much on behalf of liberty! It is well known how the former regime persecuted this courageous pamphleteer for whom vice held no secrets. He depicted the corrupt morals of the aristocrats and they pursued him with their hate. Finally, it is well known how on the first days of July he managed to direct the holy outrage of the people against the Bastille. It is possible to see in him, in the name of justice one must see in him, the instigator of the events of 14 July, on which day liberty was born! He, however, did not benefit from the work for which he had laboured and was not liberated from the prison in which the tyrant, having tried to deprive him of the gratitude of the people, kept him incarcerated for a further three months. After which, he gave himself up to good works and the welfare of the public. Now the merciless drums of Santerre have sounded for him. Let us salute without bitterness this death which snatches him from our admiration and from the service of the Revolution. He will undoubtedly find there the peace which his restlessness, his anxiety and his passionate nature would never allow him to experience here. And let the Supreme Being, the goddess Reason in whose arms he shall fall asleep, console him for the troubles to which he has been subjected here on earth in order to ensure the triumph of justice. The Republic, from now on relatively secure, will teach its children by his example and welcome his memory to its glorious annals.

Madness! You did not salute the Marquis's lucid death. Tyranny regained its sway over the mind and he died during the course of the monotonous fourteen-year-long roll of the Empire's drums.

Tombs and graves! Raised on a Saint-Malo reef among the spume or dug deep in a virgin forest by lost children, granite tombs, tombs decorated with box trees and artificial wreaths, cold tombs in pantheons, despoiled tombs near the pyramids which quiver with faith and souls, natural graves, graves fashioned in the burning lava of erupting volcanoes or in the still waters of the depths of the oceans, tombs and graves, you are the ridiculous proof of human petty-mindedness. No one has ever put anything except the dead in tombs and graves: so much the worse for them and all those who would irrevocably attach their despicable souls to a despicable carcass.

But, finally, it is you I salute, you whose existence grants a supernatural joy to my days. I loved you even because of your name. I have followed the path which your shadow traced in a melancholy desert where I abandoned all my friends. And now, when I thought I had fled you, I find you again, and the blazing sun of moral solitude illuminates your face and body once more.

Farewell, world! If I must follow you to the abyss, follow you I shall! Night after night I shall contemplate your eyes shining in the darkness, your face barely lit but visible in the clear night of Paris, thanks to the reflection of street-lamps in the room. I shall contemplate your tender eyes, touching in their dampness, until the dawn which, awakening the condemned men with the finger of a ghost in a top hat, will remind us that the hour of contemplation has passed, and that one must laugh and speak and suffer — not the oppressive and consoling midday sun above deserted beaches directly facing the stunning sky traversed by playful clouds, but the harsh law of constraint, the prison of elegance, the pseudo-discipline of human relations and the inexpressible dangers of the fragmentation of dream by utilitarian existence.

And if I must follow you to the abyss, follow you I shall!

You are not the passer-by, but the one who remains. The notion of eternity is linked to my love for you. No, you are not the passer-by nor the strange pilot guiding the adventurer through the labyrinth of desire. You have opened to me the country of passion itself. I lose myself in your thoughts more surely than in a desert. And even as I write these lines, I have still not confronted my image of you with your "reality". You are not the passer-by but the eternal lover, whether you wish it or not. Painful joy of the passion aroused by meeting you. I suffer, but my suffering is dear to me, and if I hold myself in any esteem, it is because I have encountered you in my blind rush towards the shifting horizons.

XII. *Possession of the Dream*

There was a large crowd, and an elegant one, that day on the beach at Nice. The inhabitants of the most elegant towns on the coast, such as Cannes, had made their way in large numbers to this most cosmopolitan of cities. The reason being that it had been shrouded in mystery ever since the arrival of an ostentatious but enigmatic traveller. This traveller had rented a villa at Cimiez and from that moment there had been a continuous stream of parties thrown by him, and ostentation. One day he had strewn the Promenade des Anglais with a multitude of camellias and anemones intermingled with the rarest algae, harvested at enormous expense from the depths of the equatorial oceans, and entire trees of white coral. On another occasion he had distributed thousands of strange gold coins of an unknown denomination — on their obverse side was engraved an unintelligible symbol; and on the reverse there shone the number 43 — that no one had been able to explain.

This time there was talk of a party called *the marvellous fishing trip*. Magnificent fishing-boats painted in white would ferry the guests out to predetermined points not far from the coast and there everyone was supposed to cast his or her net into the water and haul in an astonishing catch determined in advance by the enigmatic nabob.

On the hot sands and glittering pebbles, there were the duchesses of Pavia and Polynesia, the royal princes of Sweden, Norway, Romania and Albania, innumerable counts, marquises, viscounts and barons, and those representatives of the aristocracy of the commonalty as were most in the public eye, captains of industry or the arts, who in France are on such intimate terms with each other, and finally the traditional nobility, whose members were obliged during the course of the festivities to fight with princes of metallurgy and kings of finance.

And who was the organiser of all this revelry? No one had ever seen him. Some declared he was a maharajah, others affirmed he was an American banker, though none were in a position to prove their claims. Everyone listened to their dreams and explained the mystery in the romantic terms which suited them best. The villa at Cimiez was closed to everyone without exception. In order to counter the risk of intruders, the Madagascan servants who made up the retinue of the rich eccentric spread the rumour that high-tension cables ran around the top of the wall and across the park, forming an insurmountable system of defence which would trap those imprudent enough to test it for themselves like flies in a spider's web. But anyone audacious enough — and sufficiently favoured by chance — to reach the villa on the morning of the fishing party would have seen a young man wearing a mask issuing his last instructions. Naked Malaysian slaves loaded with jewels, negro boys also naked and bearing rare fish, caskets filled with amber or diamonds or pearls, precious vestiges of former civilisations, were all to be secretly conveyed by means of eighty diving-bells to the points where the fishing-boats would anchor. As the nets were cast, they would immediately be filled, some with women, some with negroes, others with jewels, these constituted the magnificent presents destined for the guests. The divers who were in charge of supervising the operation were grouped around Lord X, as he was called along the whole coast where his exploits astonished the population. On his order, they donned their diving-suits except for the helmet. And it was by no means a common sight to see this elegant dandy in the black mask giving his instructions to these determined-looking men in their baroque diving apparel.

Let us return to the party in preparation on the beach. If we examine the richly dressed throng closely, we will discover Louise Lame, the music-hall chanteuse, and a number of members of the Sperm Drinkers' Club.

The atmosphere was unsettled. Under a warm sun, these men — some of whom had been admitted, despite their self-evident stupidity, by privilege of blood or fortune, others, of comparable, though perhaps better concealed stupidity because of their supposed genius — rendered all the more evident the charms of the beautiful women present, with their adorable bodies, thrilling eyes and astonishingly luxurious wardrobes.

Three orchestras on the sea-wall played Hawaiian tunes, blues and rag-time. But no one knew that the immensely wealthy man who had invited them all was actually amongst them. Corsair Sanglot, affecting the air of a young clubman, strolled from group to group, greeted by those whom he had met at a previous party, chatting to others whom he had encountered by chance around the gaming tables or over a round of golf.

At last, the boats approached the beach. Sturdy sailors, their trouser legs rolled up, carried those who were going fishing on board. The vessels, painted in bright colours, adorned with flowers, let their engines gently throb. On the sterns were painted delightful names such as: *Le Zéphyr-Étoilé, La Chute-des-Léonides, La Mère-du-Sillage-Fatal*, and others. The boats, fully laden, remained motionless for a moment then, on a brief order, they began to make for the open sea, leaving eighty parallel wakes behind them. The women's light dresses bloomed in the sunshine. Beneath the transparent water the shadows of startled fish could be seen flitting over the smooth sand.

The breeze carried the sound of the orchestra out to the boats. A dense crowd made up of those who had not been invited watched the spectacle from the top of the sea-wall.

There was much laughter among those fishing for treasure. Shouts were exchanged between boats, hands were dangled in the water, perfumed cigarettes were smoked.

The more alert of the guests pointed out to each other two well-dressed gentlemen of serious demeanour: two of the Sûreté's best detectives whose job it was to mingle with the guests in order to prevent any thefts from being committed, either by the Malaysian sailors who manned the boats or by any criminals who might have been attracted by the lure of the easily pilfered riches that these frivolous women wore on their bodies and the carefree young men carried in their pockets.

Corsair Sanglot, at the back of one of the boats, was dreaming, Louise Lame and the German music-hall chanteuse, huddling together, felt an inexplicable sense of anxiety.

Suddenly, the engines stopped throbbing. They had arrived at the marvellous fishing-ground. Some of the nets had already been cast when on the horizon there appeared a thin white line of spume coming towards them. At first no one paid any attention. But one of the sailors who saw it immediately shouted: "Sharks! Sharks!"

And sharks they were, drawing closer by the second with rapid flicks of their tails and, from the sea-wall where the whole of Nice was gathered, a great cry of anguish arose. The boats scattered, but the sharks were almost upon them. Suddenly, they dived. A long, heart-stopping moment passed, then the waves began to turn red. Red with blood. Then several of the sharks resurfaced and ploughed straight into the boats. It is then that Corsair Sanglot...

NOTES

1. Robert Desnos's dedication is generally believed to be to the music-hall and cabaret chanteuse Yvonne George (1896-1930). Although she was not attracted to men, he was crazy about her from about 1925 onwards. Some of the evocative remarks about the nature of love in the novel are perhaps addressed to her.

2. Prince Pierre Bonaparte's shooting of Victor Noir in a fit of rage in 1870 provoked one of the biggest anti-Bonapartist demonstrations in the last days of the Empire.

3. Mary Ann Caws explains this character, and the long footnote which follows soon after in the novel, in these terms: "At twenty-one [Bébé Cadum] engages in epic battle with another signboard figure, the giant Bibendum Michelin. Thus the cliché emblem of Michelin tyres on French signboards and guidebooks serves as the banal origin of an extended elaboration in a poetic vein; the instantly understandable reference to the places in which the thirsty voyager is refreshed (Bibendum: to be drunk, a fat and bouncy figure) is the literal *source* of the verbal profusion. This play of names permits lengthy linguistic spoofs and farcical nonsense, as the Bébé becomes a baby who drinks, the bastard son of Bibendum, as Bibendum himself gives birth to an army of tyres, and so on." (*The Surrealist Voice of Robert Desnos*, University of Massachusetts Press, 1977, p.46.)

4. *Nous n'irons plus au bois, les lauriers sont coupés.* Popular French children's song.

5. A popular preacher (1802-1861) during the Romantic period who refused to abandon his political liberalism.

6. Feminist and revolutionary, her fatal beauty was considered by many royalists to have intoxicated the masses during the opening days of the French Revolution. She died insane in 1807.

7. I.e. Joan of Arc.

8. Prince of Caria (377-353). He is remembered for his wealth — and the tomb his widow is reputed to have had constructed in his honour.

9. The Club des Feuillants was formed by the moderate majority of deputies who left the Jacobin Club in 1791. Their premises, on the Rue Saint-Honoré, were formerly a monastery.

10. French seafarer and explorer (1790-1842) whose tomb at Montparnasse Cemetery is, in fact, to be found next to that of the Desnos family.

11. The Bourbons returned to the French throne in 1814.

12. Exalted Catholic who was told by God in 1610 to assassinate Henri IV.

13. Louis XIV's somewhat reluctant mistress from 1661 onwards. Exiled herself to Chaillot in 1671 but was fetched back.

14. Salacious song published in *Littérature* (n.s.), Nos. 11-12, 15 Oct. 1923, pp.1-2. Max Jacob is said to be the author (Henri Béhar, *André Breton. Le grand indésirable*, Calmann-Lévy, 1990, p.149).

15. Literally: "wrinkly-arse".

16. It was in the gardens of this church that the first event of the "Dada Season 1921" took place on 14 April. The visit was something of a failure because of lack of preparation and bad weather. Michel Sanouillet has suggested that the visit was organised as much for its convenient location and pleasant gardens as from anti-clerical motives — the same would seem to hold true here.

17. Baron and public benefactor (1733-1820) who founded numerous awards, including a prize in 1783 for an act of virtue committed by a poor Frenchman, to be chosen by the Académie Française.

18. A clown legendary at the time for his disguises and quick costume changes.

19. After being freed in 1790 on the orders of the National Assembly, the Marquis de Sade is claimed by some to have participated actively in the early stages of the Revolution. While it is certainly true that he joined the Section des Piques based around the Place Vendôme, the precise extent to which he may be considered to have taken part in Revolutionary activities is still not settled.

Mourning for Mourning

These ruins are situated on the banks of a winding river. The town must have been quite sizable at some time in history. A few large buildings, a network of underground galleries and a number of towers of bizarre construction may still be seen. In these sunny and deserted squares fear takes hold of us. But despite our fear, nobody, absolutely nobody, approaches us. The ruins are uninhabited. To the south-west, a tall edifice of some kind, open-sided and made of metal, has been erected, the purpose of which remains uncertain. It looks as if it is on the brink of toppling over, for it leans out at an angle above the river:

"Strange diseases, curious customs — where is the bell's clapper of love leading me? Amongst these stones I can find no vestige of what I am seeking. The imperturbable and ever-changing mirror reveals to me only myself. Is the deserted town, a Sahara, the place where our magnificent encounter must necessarily occur? I watched from afar the arrival of beautiful millionairesses with their caravans of camels brocaded in gold. I waited for them, tormented and unmoved. Before they reached me they turned into shrivelled old women coated in dust, their drivers transformed into dotards. I have become accustomed to bursting into laughter at these funeral rites which serve me for a landscape. I have lived whole eternities in dark tunnels deep in the mines. I have fought with marble-white vampires but despite my clever words I was really always all alone in the padded cell where I tried my best to give birth to fire through the impact of my hard brain against the incredibly soft walls and to recall the memory of imaginary hips.

"That which I did not know, I invented better than any eighteen-carat America, than the cross or a wheelbarrow. Love! Love! I will summon you no more to describe the humming attributes of aircraft engines. I will speak of you tritely, for the commonplace is better calculated to set off the extraordinary adventure I have been planning since my earliest words of whatever gender. As is fitting, I have taught old men to respect my black hair, and women to adore my limbs, but with respect to the latter I have always conserved my extensive yellow dominion where I ceaselessly confront the metallic vestiges of the high, inexplicable, pyramid-shaped construction in the distance. Love, would you condemn me to make of these ruins a ball of clay in which to carve my own likeness, or should I draw it forth as a weapon from my own eyes? In that case, which eye should I employ for this purpose and would it not be more advantageous for me to use both in order to fashion a pair of lovers that I can blindly rape, a new Homer standing on the Pont des Arts whose sinister arches I should gropingly undermine, at the risk of being abandoned, incapable of directing my steps towards the great yellow expanses teeming with sunshine where muskets stand guard over dead sentries. Love, would you condemn me to become the guardian spirit of these ruins and shall I live henceforth forever young amidst what little of the moon these white ruins allow me to glimpse?"

It was at this moment that they appeared. Pilotless planes weaving rings of smoke round enormous immobile airborne lighthouses perched on cliffs of ever-changing shapes, fanned out like an apotheosis. It was at this moment that they appeared:

The first wore a three-cornered hat, black tails and a white waistcoat; the second leg-of-mutton sleeves and a ruff; and the third a low-cut black silk chemisette that slipped from left to right and from right to left to reveal alternately, as far as the first hint of her breasts, two white but slightly swarthy shoulders.

I possess in high degree the arrogance of my sex. The humiliation of a man before a woman will either render me feverish and taciturn for days at a time or produce a white rage within me that I can only assuage by studied cruelties inflicted upon certain animals or objects; none the less, I seek out these inflammatory sights which occasionally force me to block my ears and shut my eyes.

I do not believe in God, but I have a sense of the infinite. No one has a more religious nature than me. I run up against unanswerable questions all the time. The questions that I acknowledge to myself are all unanswerable. Others would only be posed by people lacking in imagination and do not interest me.

These ruins are situated on the banks of a winding river. There is nothing special about the climate here. To the south-west, a tall edifice of some kind, open-sided and made of metal, has been erected, the purpose of which remains uncertain.

✳

One day or one night or some other time the doors will shut: this prediction is self-evident to all. I lie in wait for the prophet at the bend in the black road between the green fields beneath the birch-grey sky. He appears, dressed presentably, clean-shaven and wearing gloves.

"The great immigration is for the day after tomorrow. The ecliptic will become a tiny violet spiral. There will be fir trees. They will cross the oceans and the continents. Near Dieppe they will encounter icebergs and the ice floe sailing side by side in opposite directions, then tropical creepers and violets will invade everywhere. The Earth will have two verdant poles and a glacial chastity belt."

But what will man have to say when confronted by these great mobilisations of the mineral and vegetable worlds, being himself the unstable plaything of the whirlwind's farcical games and of the marriage between the lesser elements and the chasms which separate the resounding words?

The spiral spring of the past squeezes, celebrates and mixes together its photographic plates. O silken locks of Théroigne de Méricourt so dearly beloved by scheming lovers!

I watch the swallows and their imaginary aerodromes where for the last few green marsh-mallow days mis-shapen arrows have described multicoloured arabesques to the great delight of the tiny aeronautical serpents whose clearly audible hissing informs the lost explorer of an unknown street in the centre of a distant town that the woman in the sky-blue robes is rapidly approaching despite her high heels, and each of her naked breasts, encircled by the twin haloes of St Peter and St Paul, is clearly visible through the gaping holes cut into the satin of her high bodice.

The nature of the relationship between the flight paths of the swallows, the arrows and the flying snakes, to the woman in the sky-blue robes, is comparable to the conjunction of three sunbeams reflected by polished mirrors made of precious metal. Should one put one's finger there, a round blister scorches its indelible mark. But as for the woman in the sky-blue robes (is it still the same one?), I never tire of speaking of her and disguising her by hiding from your eyes the violet lobster claws which serve her in place of feet.

The tiny snakes have whispered it into my ear; I utter aloud two letters at random: the initials of the woman in the sky-blue robes, with naked breasts and lobster claws instead of feet.

At the bend in the road I met Charles V whose acquaintance I have long wanted to make.

He passed close by me, dressed in black velvet robes. In his right hand, he was holding the dead body of a bird whose species I was unable to determine, a drawing-room variety, a canary or an albatross; in his left hand, he held a minute pot of nasturtiums.

Nearing me, he said:

"The day on which all your friends disappear at a stroke or on which the whole Earth disappears and all that is on it save you, on that day when you are alone, they will think you are dead; but it will be them. When a man dies, the universe dies, and there are many men amongst men. The woman in the sky-blue robes is approaching, a woman like any other, you will have had enough of her soon enough, you have the time to run and free yourself from artificial gravity."

The nasturtiums are blooming in the stream.

It is raining jewels and daggers.

Once upon a time there was a crocodile. The crocodile fed upon bathers wearing black swimming-costumes but spared those in pink swimming-costumes. All the same, there were so many bathing beauties in black swimming-costumes. This crocodile is also a bracelet. I gave this bracelet to the woman in the sky-blue robes. In exchange, she gave me her robes. I watched her leave naked in the night between the trees.

✳

"Never did he offer up sacrifice in the ephemeral light of candles." I paused a long time over this sentence which is to be found on page thirty-two of the complete works of Bossuet[1] and the austere physiognomy of the preacher, with his two wings like a white auk, rose up before the prismatic binocular of my imagination. A few days later I was drinking spirits on the terrace of a café while watching with my right eye a woman who was as white and pink as the queen of the ice floes and with my left eye a Prussian-blue woman with translucent eyes and lips as pale as Venetian glass who was reading a letter written on red paper.

The magic of colours, which for painters is not yet a commonplace, was preserved in my tea spoon. I had, in fact, dipped it in best-quality petrol. Colours are magical, not by the sole virtue of being seen through the eyes of a palette scraper but because they are intrinsically so. I was debating writing an article on this subject, treating it from an esoteric point of view, when I noticed that the woman on the left had become a pretty joint of lamb in a collar of Mechlin lace. A man was imperturbably carving it. Tiny white streams like milk yet as radiant as diamonds poured from this soft flesh into a champagne flute. This outdated receptacle grew increasingly larger as the liquid continued to flow into it such that there was never more than a drop in the bottom which was reflected in each of the facets cut in the goblet. Thanks to the sunshine, each of these sharply-focused reflections showed my face and the foot sheathed in the dark-blue stockings worn by the woman on the right. The whole image expanded considerably without becoming distorted in proportion to the increase in size of the glass and I observed that my own skin, which is normally relatively delicate and agreeable to the touch, assumed on this scale the aspect of a solid block of steel. The woman on the right stood up. I stood up as well in order to follow her, but I was dazzled and the reflections of my face danced before me like a hail of bullets fired by invisible hunters. The woman that I was following had a slight limp. But I could not keep up with her. At the top of an uphill road she disappeared. I broke into a run. When I arrived at the summit she was no larger than a point near the bottom of the street on the other side. She continued a little while further and turned into a side-street. I was left alone to examine the cross-roads above which there shone a green street-lamp. A bus went past. It was completely empty. Even though there was nobody waiting, it came to a halt. The conductor rang the bell, the drowsy motor roared into life and the luminous vehicle drove off into the twilight until it too disappeared.

Bossuet! Bossuet! You would no doubt have passed for a decent enough bloke had you not lent the resounding weight of your voice to the service of established authority and empty principles instead of preaching a revolutionary ethics more preoccupied with the insoluble mysteries of the individual than with the arbitrary riddles of a senile metaphysics and a hoary religion. A strong wind buffets the violet clouds which open to reveal a woman's leg and occasionally the sleeper is awoken at midnight by his candle or the electric light. It sputters and crackles, and lights of its own volition. The man studies the strange shadows for a moment which have so transformed his walls, he rises, hastily throws a coat over his pyjamas and makes for the cross-roads where the woman on the right, as pretty as a thief, had disappeared. He watches the empty buses pass until dawn. The piercing eyes of the courageous decipher the illuminated inscription above the driver's head. It reads: "CORRIDOR". If he has any feelings and is anxious, he will hold his peace, even during love-making, or else he will seek in the key of dreams a utilitarian explanation for his nocturnal adventure. He will wait a long time for a stroke of luck or set out to search for it beyond his native town without suspecting that I tirelessly count the illuminated coins which comprise the hidden treasure of the masters of the arcane under the thirty-second flagstone of the street along which the empty buses pass towards "*Corridor*". Behind him, on the hill of white camels and gasometers, Bossuet raises his white index finger towards the thunder. A short while ago, I placed a top hat over his white hair. The wind blows without even extinguishing the tiny red lanterns across the barricaded roads. The nocturnal passer-by may walk without fear; if I do not assassinate him at the next bend, he will sleep easily in his bed or placidly procreate with his idiotic wife. He will, no doubt, always remain ignorant of the majestic bishop who wears eight moonbeams on his head.

Have you got change for this coin? Nobody in the world can change my coin.

*

"Kill him! kill him!" screams the audience. I could see nothing of the tragic spectacle. Half-naked girls, strong men, young lads — they came and they went. But the monotonous, disturbing procession of people motivated by the same fears and the same desires does not produce drama. That resides in the fate of a shutter half torn from its hinges which the lugubrious winter winds repeatedly shook as they laboured to rip it off completely in order, no doubt, to install it in some unknown window in the sky, probably the very same one at which every day at ten or three o'clock a beautiful blonde, stripped to the waist, silently waters a pot of geraniums while mentally comparing the blueness of her own eyes with the until then incomparable blueness of the sky deeper than a sea plied by the largest vessels whose cruel bows cut deep into the waves and remind the sleeping sharks amongst the coral that they have long since eaten all the fish to be found in these oceanic regions and that they are still hungry. The splash of tails then transforms the calm surface on which Gauguin's islands lie dreaming and the women, dream-like stars bent over their own reflections at the portholes, the red eyes of the steamer, ask themselves what tremendous passion suddenly stirs these tarnished silver underbellies, these fearsome quadruple jaws with their soft red palates and dorsal fins whose colour recalls the peaceful sofas of fashionable smoking-rooms without it ever occurring to them that this very construction specially assembled to transport them to distant places was alone responsible for awakening these aquatic monsters, making their fins ring with the urge to travel and endowing their healthy frames with the unexpected agility required for them to head for temperate zones, whether arctic or tropical, to seek new prey, and steeling them for the dishonourable slaughter of myriads of pink shrimps in shallow waters.

In the end, the wind carried off the shutter. The sun made use of it to flay with alternate stripes of sunlight and shadow the crowd clamouring: "Kill him! kill him!" in the street in which I vainly stand on tiptoe to discover the cause of so much hatred, while still following out of *"The Corner of my Eye"* the baroque flight of the shutter being supernaturally borne away by the wind towards, without any doubt whatsoever, the mysterious window. My double vigil was not in vain. The shutter slipped on to the invisible hinges of a window at which a gorgeous brunette with limpid eyes appeared at the very moment when, naked except for blindfolded breasts, she triumphantly escaped the reach of the crowd — who were still cowardly clamouring for an execution — before they even managed to place their little fingers on the white shoulders and majestic neck of she who, from the window high in the sky, studied their useless antics. Eventually she noticed me and said: "I know who you are yet I am unable to say who we are. The ridiculous conjugal convention of the verb separates and unites us. I have marvellous eyes and enough jewellery to damn me. Look at my arms and my neck. An indescribable love is welling up inside you even as I speak. I am the dark Beauty and the blonde Beauty. The triumphant beauty without beauty. I am You and you are I. Clusters of plums hang from my fingertips. A heart is like a little pea which will germinate absurdly into its destiny: an anonymous accompaniment to the mortal remains of a wild duck in a richly-coloured sauce on a silver plate."

✳

Regularly, after every revolution, the flags of the former regime flutter forgotten above the buildings, which will shortly be put to new uses, then fly away like storks, and naked women walk about in groups of four or five before sunrise in that uneasy hour during which the belfries tremble with the confused vibrations of bells. Although naked, they continue to circulate under the approving gaze of policemen and watch the emigration of the birds in their gaudy regalia and, occasionally, one of them manages to claim possession as it passes as an oriflamme, which may be glorious, if we are to believe the curators, both diverting it from its course and distracting it from its function so as to attire herself in its alluring colours. Losing all sense of dignity, the woman so attired watches the lights of her crown of dreams fade away, and while her eyebrows, abandoning that rectitude which formerly characterised them, conform to the rules of the arc, healthy muscles swell her harmonious frame. She walks straight to the nearest lamp-post and there, testifying to the fact that no gallows nor Golgotha were more tragic, she vanishes into the air first like swan's-down, then like a puff of smoke, then like a glance, a reflection in a mirror, the memory of a perfume.

That is why the city streets, which are congested and noisy an hour later, are deserted for the final hour before dawn.

Listen to the drums and the shouts: the baleful circulation of a powerful motor-car augurs the next Revolution. Men will be guillotined, flags will fly away like storks but the unguillotinable women will disappoint, leaving the sympathetic hangmen up on their bloody scaffolds lost in thought.

✳

The North Star sends this telegram to the South Star: "Decapitate red comet and violet comet immediately; they are betraying you. — North Star." The South Star's face clouds over and she bows her dark-haired head on her charming neck. The female regiment of comets caper at her feet; pretty canaries in a cage of eclipses. Must she deprive her moving treasures of her beautiful red one and her beautiful violet one? These two comets which at five o'clock delicately raise their taffeta skirts to reveal their lunar knees? The beautiful red one with the moist lips is a friend of adulterers whom more than one abandoned lover has discovered curled up in his bed, her long lashes feigning a swoon; the beautiful red one, moreover, with her dark-blue dresses, her dark-blue eyes, and her dark-blue heart is like a lost jellyfish far from every shore in a warm stream haunted by ghost ships. And what about the beautiful violet one! The beautiful violet one with the flame-coloured hair, the lovely hat and veil, and scarlet earlobes, who eats sea urchins, and whose remarkable crimes have slowly speckled her dress, her precious dress, with tears of blood so admirable and admired throughout the heavens. Should she strangle them with her fingers of diamonds, she, the charming South Star, and follow the perfidious advice of the North Star, the magical, adorable and seductive North Star, whose nipples at the points of her breasts, warm and white as the reflection of the sun at noon, have been replaced by diamonds?

Female pilot lights, violet and red comets, pilot lights of a ghost ship, whither do you guide your cargo of whores and skeletons whose fabulous couplings carry the consolation of eternal love to the regions you traverse? Seductresses! The veil of the violet one is a fishing-net and the red one's knee serves as a compass. The whores of the ghost ship are eighty-four in number. Here are some of their names:

Rose, Mystery, Embrace, Midnight, Police, Direct, Crazy, And Hearts and Spades, From Me, From Afar, Enough, The Gold, The Green Glass, The Murmur, The Galandine, and The Mother-of-Kings who has experienced barely sixteen of those which are considered the best years. For want of a cause, the skeletons of *The Armada* join battle with those of *The Medusa*.

High above, in the sky, float scattered jellyfish.

Before she becomes a comet, the South Star sends this telegram to the North Star. "Plunge the sky into your icebergs! Justice has been done! — South Star."

Perfidious North Star!

Seductive South Star!

How adorable!

How adorable!

✸

On the table a glass and a bottle are laid out in memory of a fair-haired virgin who in this room experienced the disturbing menstrual wound for the first time and who, raising her right arm towards the ceiling and pointing her left towards the window, was able to make triangles of moving pigeons flutter in the air to her heart's content. Below, down where the burning sands of the desert jealously hide a gentle blue dolman on a manikin of white bones, she knelt and prayed the heavens to change into a scarf with which she could cover her shoulders, shoulders which to tell the truth were slightly bony but extremely delicate when one thinks of the blows of the whip which will not fail to rain down on her back and clenched buttocks, far away from here at the end of a seam in the silver mines of Baikal in the time of the Tsar.

While waiting, the fair-haired virgin dips her blonde tresses in my coffee; it is midday; the statutory litre of wine which has been deposited next to the ribbed glass in front of me turns into a dove. The coffee turns into tea, the fair-haired virgin grows a little pale; from now on she will sing sweeter than the nightingale. The bell rings: in his ribbed velvet garb the forensic expert comes in. He takes a seat. He liberates the dove imprisoned in the bottle, he turns over the glass which becomes an egg-timer, kisses the fair-haired virgin on the lips. He accuses me of murder. Enter... who? Two policemen... carrying handcuffs!

That, Your Honour, ladies and gentlemen of the jury, is how I come to be here. Your ridiculous accoutrements lead me to believe, alas, that the reign of Henri III has not yet come to an end. The statutory litre becomes a crown. The glass turns into a glass eye for your empty socket. The police doctor will invent a sleep machine which will abolish awakening.

As for me, I will turn into a giant clad in iron and gold more supple than silk. You might have taken me for an eagle, but eagles have wings and in my name this letter auguring an irreparable fall does not figure. By dint of working the mines, the Earth will be made hollow. Personally, I sleep on a glass table, you are imitation doves in a state of mortal sin. The flood would fit in my statutory litre, and I enjoin you to render unto me that which is Caesar's.

✳

Down below, where a skeleton serves as a dummy for a soft blue dolman, the fair-haired virgin increases her pace across the desert sands. And each grain of sand communicates the news to its neighbour; this news precedes the fair-haired virgin and runs concentric circles around her; at the very spot where her foot lands, the footprint frequently obliterates the news contained in the numerous grains of sand to be found in the none the less tiny space which is occupied by a single one of her footprints. The news spreads all round the world. The quick-sands of *St Michel*, the green ones of the *Kalahari*, those of the hour-glass which have long been deprived of air, those of beaches and those which, like telluric tears, are encased in a sheath of tarmac, the road's beautiful dress. The news, furious all the same at being disclosed, rises up beyond the horizon and its hand threatens the small fair-haired virgin ever so tiny in the middle of the vast desert where the wind, still deeply moved by the sighs of Memnon, asks itself what is this soft blue dolman floating about a skeleton. The fair-haired virgin arrives at her destination before the news and when the latter arrives in turn it finds a notice which reads:

LEBLOND

Military outfitters

and has no choice but to continue its journey against the hubbub of the whispering sands.

What occurred between the dolman, the skeleton and the fair-haired virgin? It appears that, daughter of Eve, she had put on the dolman whilst the skeleton sank back into the earth with a whistle. Once she was clothed in the dolman, the desert squadrons asked her what orders she had? And she, what could she say but suddenly command the fearsome gallop of two thousand dromedaries first across the Sahara, then through all the stables of the world before stopping outside those of John John, the renowned racehorse owner. Aesthetically displeasing sight! Two thousand camels next to thirty thoroughbreds! The racecourses were given over to cows and John John, the owner, the man who never went fishing, declared his faith in the new-found speed. A red car drove John John and the fair-haired virgin to the country where they sought refuge in a sumptuous cottage with their only desire being to end their days in fasting and abstinence. Fasting? What pride: they will grow old. As for abstinence, that was prohibited, yes prohibited, just like hunting and fishing and baldness. There now, charming fair-haired virgin, off you go… all the way to adultery.

*

The fire that consumed Sodom and Johann Hus and the cigarette stump that I have just discarded burns over the seas and marshes, on the edges of cemeteries, in the smoke of locomotives, in the portholes of liners.

On the sea-bed, starfish talk to oysters and to the wreckage. Their words, transmitted to the coral by the usual vibrations of the water, do not give rise to the slightest delay in the fabulous timetable of the tides. The starfish remembered, however, that she had once been Venus taking her regular stroll along the invisible paths of the firmament where the terrifying crocodiles prosper that the storm sometimes lets loose on the uninhabited cities of this fauna since the last day of the deluge. She remembered that she was Icarus and that this was the very spot where she had fallen, how she had vainly tried to emerge from the sea, which is what gave rise to the absurd myth of the profane birth of the goddess of love, and that overcome by her heaviness and cramp she had had to settle for a resting-place on the damp sands of the depths. Poor star shining out of reach of the fishermen, she stretches voluptuously her five delicate arms and makes the oyster finally release the pearl which time and illness had given him.

Strange indeed was the dialogue of the starfish and the oyster. The pearl rolled as far as the wreck which barely noticed and the starfish completed her stretch. She did this on clear October mornings, she the perfect mistress and sensual lover, when, as he unloaded cart-loads of roses, the colourless assassin who was following her finally dropped the deadly knife into the mahogany-coloured stream.

The starfish sleeps now.

The oyster has closed its sturdy lid, which becomes encrusted with barnacles, over its despoiled stickiness.

Only the wreckage stirs. It rose to the surface with a pearl. The pearl rolled around the bridge, the pearl took the helm, the navigated wreckage reached coastal waters; an estuary offered its mouth barricaded by the encounter of fresh water and salt water; the vessel sailed up the estuary against the tide. The riverside dwellers witnessed that night the will-o'-the-wisp and a miraculous brilliance to their pipes and lanterns. Standing at their windows, they saw a white furrow mysteriously crawling upstream. They thought it was the moon and went to bed untroubled.

Tomorrow, the starfish will recall an anchor and the oyster a porthole. They will be amazed by the disappearance of the wreck on the back of which the word MARVEL may be made out and will continue their mutual mute contemplation.

And yet, how surprised will be the guide to the Ardennes Forest to see deadly nightshade flowering on paths now frequented only by ferns. He will find a boat planted in the middle of the trees with a pearl at the helm, a pearl which will order him to die and which he will obey.

The man in the soft blue dolman, the huntsman in the bar where the fair-haired virgin is a regular, the bare-armed huntsman will chop down oak trees not far from there.

And the pearl, eternally transfixed to the wheel, will be amazed that the boat remains forever immobile under an ocean of fir trees unaware of the magnificent destiny that was bestowed on her equals in civilised lands, in towns where bar huntsmen have dolmans the colour of the sky.

✳

William the Conqueror, the same one who discovered the law of the attraction of boats, William the Conqueror is buried not far from here. A gravedigger is sitting on a tomb. He has already reached the age of eighty-four since the beginning of this story. He does not have to wait for long. A greenish light emanates from a molehill at his feet which hardly surprises him, accustomed as he is to silence, forgetfulness and murder and knowing as he does of life only the soft humming that accompanies the perpendicular fall of the sun when the hands of the clock press one against another and tired of waiting for night to fall call in vain with their prophetic cry a dozen times repeated for the violet pageant of spectres and phantoms detained far from here in a chance bed between love and mystery, at the feet of liberty, arms outspread against the wall. The gravedigger recalls that at this very spot he once, with barely-twitching ears, killed the queen mole whose huge skin clad each of his mistresses in turn with a suit of iron armour a thousand times more redoubtable than Nessus's famous shirt and against which his kisses took on the consistency of ice and glass, and in whose tethers he watched for night after night the slow and steady loss of his hair endowed with an infernal life. The most illustrious funerals were prolonged while awaiting his arrival. When he got there, those attending had grown old. Some of them, including even the undertakers and the weeping women, were dead. He threw them pell-mell into the grave reserved for a single, glorious corpse before anybody dared to protest, so great was the respect that the green halo of his hair imposed on the mourners. But now, on the midnight anniversary of the death of William the Conqueror, his last remaining hair has departed leaving a hole, a black hole in his skull, while the green light radiates from the molehill.

And now, preceded by the grating sound of locks being forced, comes the funeral of *Mystery*, followed by a battalion of keys in close formation. There they all are, all of them, those which fell into the hands of spies, those which the murderous lover broke inside the lock as he went away, those that the avenger threw into the river after definitively closing the door on retaliation, the jailers' golden keys stolen by the prisoners, the keys of towns sold to the enemy by fair-haired virgins, by the fair-haired virgin, the diamond keys of chastity belts, the keys of bankers' safes rifled without their knowledge by adventurers, and those which the ideal young conqueror draws noiselessly from the lock to peep at the fair-haired virgin preparing for bed.

And while the skies resounded with the noise of divine locks closed in haste, the gravedigger, the gravedigger died beneath this cannibalistic accumulation of keys on the tomb of William the Conqueror, while inside the molehill, in the green light, the obsequies took place for the golden ant, the lock of intelligences.

✳

1, 2, 3, 4, 5, 6, 7, 8, 9, nought, chanted the children to the time marked by the schoolmistress, the fair-haired virgin schoolmistress who for the last few days has been wearing a soft blue dolman. But the fair-haired thoughts of the virgin schoolmistress were a thousand miles away from the classroom strangely decorated with sheep and camel bones; she was following the movements of a bluebottle as it made its way towards the bedroom in which the lover she so desired was resting, the lover whose physiognomy was endowed with attractive seriousness by lodestones carved into buttons for a uniform. The fly struck a path through virgin forest and stopped above a corpse, that of the lover with the lodestone buttons, and there the sound of its flight was lost in the hum of thirty similar insects equally blue and clearly visible in the evening, there to beguile the tiresomely regular meeting of Romeo and Juliet.

At that point, the fair-haired virgin abandoned the classroom in which the heads of thirty children were bent over the geometric regularity of their exercise-books. She took the path through the virgin forest where she encountered first a red tiger and then a violet tiger, they stepped aside for her without uttering a word. The fair-haired virgin still spoke to the tropical creepers like love songs and asked which path she should follow. The creepers covered in white directed her to the Field of Battle. The fair-haired virgin bent over the first dead body, it was Romeo, the second was Juliet. She abandoned her melancholy promenade there and wordlessly examined each of the buttons of the uniform. Some were splashed with blood, others with clay. (Clay which no sculptor will ever model into the adorable shape of a heart.) All of them bore strange symbols: a rooster, a playing-card, a woman's head. The eyes of the fair-haired virgin became as rigid as steel. Look out, fair-haired virgin! Your lover is close by! Don't say I didn't warn you. The magnetic buttons of the uniform ripped out the fair-haired virgin's eyes who, blinded, will henceforth wander through the fields in lamentation, her body and soul exposed to the insults of vagabonds, the kisses of cripples, the caresses of the sick, while at the first light of dawn the stretcher-bearers responsible for removing the victims of the heroic battle will tremble with fright at seeing two buttons too many on the tunic of a healthy young corpse. When they look more closely they will see that they are two eyes and their fear will become greater still. They will back away and leave the body to rot amidst the flies.

Meanwhile, in the classroom, a stick of red chalk, a stick of green chalk, a stick of yellow chalk and a stick of chalk the colour of moonlight shall wait a long time for the return of the hand which knew how to bend them to the demands of a capricious imagination. Meanwhile, dressed in earth and sky, the blind fair-haired virgin and the lover whose heart has been pierced by a sharply-pointed bullet wander the heavens. Nobody shows them the way. Nightfall, an evil black night which leads them astray from the lively fires of a forge to the pale glow of a murderous ocean.

In a cemetery there are two empty graves and two nameless tombstones fall noisily down the mountainside into a cold stream from which the children will drink without fear the following morning. Watch out, all you mothers! There will be whores amongst your daughters! There will be whores!

✳

In a northern town, there was an amazing barometer to which the storms and the rains, the sunshine and the snow used to come to receive their orders. One day, the remotest waters of all the oceans, those which lap deserted islands and those in which washerwomen do their washing, wanted to see this mysterious tyrant who regulated the equinoxes and the shipwrecks. They mounted an attack on the town. For seven days and seven nights the inhabitants defended themselves with rifle and cannon-fire against what they termed the liquid barbarians. They succumbed and on the eighth day the light of the obedient sun played across their dead bodies, presided over their decomposition and was able to see the majestic crowd of peaceful waves pay spumy tribute to the tyrannical barometer which, unmindful of the honour, reflected that far away, saved by the sacrifice of her town, the fair-haired virgin and a pirate in a pale blue dolman lay clasped together on the seaweed on the deserted ocean floor abandoned by the waters at the very moment that *The Marvel*, the liner on which they were passengers, was being engulfed.

✳

Listen. Through the thickness of night the wailing of a baby martyr tortured by its luxurious parents reaches my ears, or perhaps it is the parting cry of an angora tomcat dispatched despite its mewing on a transatlantic liner to a far-off destination and which, while the boat still follows the coast, continues to salute its wild mistresses, the crouching cats with phosphorescent eyes in place of lighthouses which threaten to lure vessels unfamiliar with this locality on to the reefs!

Listen, it is, it is neither the child-like scream of a nocturnal rape nor feline sobs, it is the sinister song of the water in the plumbing of my taps which slowly weeps on to the tombstone which serves me as a sink. The water imprisoned in the vast narrow boa which runs from one house to another hears its drips speak.

"As for me," says one, "I was once brutally propelled from a fireman's hose in order to put out a fire. What a waste of effort! The flames transformed me into a bird and I escaped towards the sky for which I was destined by the long vicissitudes I had suffered on a lake in a park where the swans were once women who, long ago, had been adulated." "Me," said the other, "I lay wallowing in a duckpond beside bodies which were turning blue and the water-lilies which lent me their delicate perfume."

From time to time, a prolonged shiver runs through the water. It is a fair-haired virgin washing herself after love-making and asking the colourless liquid to erase from her body the signs of a nightmarish struggle. Happy the drops destined for intimacy with her body, but happy also those that feel the rustle of mermaids close to the reefs or the ripping of armour-plated bows through the oceans. Another recounts how he burrowed beneath the earth before bursting out in a spring and how in that way he was permitted the vision of beautiful bathers stretching their hands towards the sky to betoken their grief before they plunged down the mountainside. Memories of coral, memories of jellyfish, memories of islands, memories of clouds, memories of girls swimming, memories following love-making, that is the ominous song sung by the water in the lead plumbing of cities. An enormous red umbrella emerges from an official edifice and deafens the urban inhabitants.

Down below, some other drops of water have shared the company of fish (who will proclaim the extraordinary importance of fish in poetry? for they evoke both fire and water and it is they who mourn the drips in the lead plumbing of cities). From time to time, the prisoners are shaken by a long loud shiver. It is the poet in the soft blue dolman who slakes his solitary thirst, it is the fair-haired virgin who dilutes her wine with water, it is the municipal sprinkler filling up before starting its morning promenade.

The frightful water drips on to the tombstone which serves me as a sink. "Water! Water! Drip no more, I am clean, drip no more. My eyes are running like you without grief or pain and I am not thirsty.

"Water, you roll too many eyes for me to look at you. I am afraid of your multiple spheres in which your memories may be clearly seen like the *Sacré Cœur* in a bone pen-holder."

But the water does not listen. It glistens. The kettle on the fire groans because the water boils and evaporates. An hour after I awake the town is dry.

"Lost pedestrian, this desert was not always so. There was once a flourishing town here, but the water departed and the sand covered it with its lustreless constellations. The tombstone on which you sit was not always thus. It was formerly the stone sink in which fresh water ran lugubriously at night filling the flat where I live with anxiety. The blue tatters of the sky were not always a flag but…"

But the pedestrian passes by and the savage sky remains without a storm. The open sky.

*

The street was a long one lined with tailors' shops. To tell the truth, none of the tradesmen were taking much money at this time of day. It was two o'clock in the morning. A recent strike had decimated the company of lamp-lighters. One of them was just finishing his round for the night and I congratulated the borough on its presence of mind in requiring its modest servants to attire themselves in pale blue for lighting up and in black when extinguishing. I walked for a long time and my shadow moved around me ominously.

One day it will doubtless stop still and that day will be my last. In the meantime, I follow the lamp-lighter wearing pale-blue overalls as he completes his round as if in a race.

An hour later, I was stopped by the fair-haired virgin. Dressed in her most beautiful clothes and wearing make-up, she had gone down to the street to try and make a bit of money by selling her body. I turned over the various aspects of this important question for a minute, I thought of old women on the coast reduced to seeking out the company of sea-horses and who slowly rise to the surface when their couplings have taken too long. The fishermen reel them in at dawn, and that makes one more grave and one less woman. I thought of the little girls from boarding-school led forty at a time into army barracks, of women who lose their dignity in bars, and of those who try to forget the hero on the screen in the convenient darkness of cinemas. Then I fell asleep.

He's asleep, said the moon.

And slowly it began to count a rosary of stars. The stars grumbled softly to themselves. The star acting as a pendant shone with a thousand fires and I wondered how much longer this incantation would last. The moon was praying! The stars grew dim one by one and the dawn made my temples grey. Crowds filled the streets, trams passed by, far away the fishermen pulled up the corpses of old women. I slept.

The surprising metamorphosis of sleep makes us equal to gods. Their actions are reduced to the same status as those of actors on a subsidised stage while we, in our dress-coats and our boxes or seats in the front stalls, applaud them. When the excitement languishes, we take their place and, just for the fun of it, risk our necks in deadly adventures.

Respect my sleep, passers-by in the street below. The great organ of the sun makes you march in step, but I will not wake until this evening when the moon begins its prayer.

I will leave for the coast where ships never land; one shall present itself, a black flag fluttering at the stern. The rocks will part.

I shall step ashore.

And my friends high in their observatories will watch the exploits of the gangs of black flags scattered across the plain, while above them the moon will say its prayer. It will count its rosary of stars and distant cathedrals will crash to the ground.

I will return only with the fair-haired virgin, the beautiful, the charming fair-haired virgin who will make the moon turn pale above the flowering apple trees.

To die! To die in a bed of watercress!

✳

In the theatre auditorium silence fell like a blanket, echoing through the rows of seats down to the front stalls: the pianist had just walked on to the stage. He took his seat before a rosewood coffin large enough to accommodate all those present, whether of obscure birth or the kind of rich people who send the undertakers' gold-braided valets scurrying at their funerals and who lie for ages in silver and taffeta mausoleums in memory of the fair-haired virgin, the one who the day they met was wearing an evening gown also of taffeta with a silver tiara in her hair.

The pianist sat down. And while the crowd listened devotedly to a rather second-rate tune, I listened to the rosewood of the piano tell me its story:

"I was already strong when savage negroes daubed in blue dragged a white man dressed in white before me. They tied this explorer to me and their arrows pierced him and made my sap spurt out, though it surprised me to see red blood pouring out of white flesh as far as my highest branches. The negroes made off with the body with the intention of selling it to his family for a lot of money, because it seems that you Europeans attach a lot of importance to this much depreciated merchandise as if we rosewood trees would buy pianos made from the salvage of our dead fathers."

A dancer who replaced the pianist prevented me from hearing the rest of the story.

I left the commonplace theatre. In the streets and roads, everywhere I wandered, there floated, seeping through the apartment windows and curtains, the story of the rosewood made into pianos.

"I was already strong when savage negroes daubed in blue, etc." I blocked my ears. When I uncovered them again, bells were ringing. It happened four hundred years ago. Pianos had conquered the town. The great assembly of these instruments at midnight on the Esplanade des Invalides was the city's main attraction.

Where will God's awful imagination lead us, O blind civilisation. We three or four clairvoyants already feel the stirrings of rebellion from below.

Here is my bed awaiting me, all marble-white and freshly ironed. A few box trees would set it off nicely.

Coffin, piano.

*

The mines of northern France, the mines of Cape Town and the mines of Baikal were having a conversation. Night was just leaving home, dressed in white and adorned with glass beads. She wandered slowly through the gardens, and the flowers — excited by the memory of the last butterfly — watched in wonder as this tall, pale figure went by, the locks of her black hair held aloft by four negro angels with red wings. She left deep footprints in the ground and glow-worms, stranded on the paths, retained the memory long afterwards of a charming foot which presented the unusual attribute of having two large toes. Night's faithful lover, Murder, appeared before his mistress, however, much to the distress of the countryside which witnessed these two pale figures wrap themselves around each other amid the wolf's-bane. Fair-haired virgin! O Night! Murder, your heaving breast attracts and repels the knife keen to strike you, handsome equerry in the sky-blue dolman, your neck inspires the respect of every gallows — as happened in London where the hangman would have slashed his wrists rather than leave you dangling in the void — and the trepidation of guillotines which fear the deep fractures that would cause so much painful damage to their blades should they drop down on your healthy muscles, despite all the efforts of Deibler,[2] the sinister archangel whose top hat is shaped like vengeance. Murder and Night walk abroad together in the streets of the town and along country roads. Dogs strain against their chains at their approach while rich farmers, waking with a start, listen to the nocturnal sound of their majestic, sinister footsteps. If they dare direct their gaze, the eyes of astronomers converge upon them, then upon a cloud which is soon dispersed, finally the silhouette of an aristocratic hand. Next morning, despite the green fields, the flourishing vines, the joyful red of the factory chimneys, they will go directly to the cemetery accompanied by the useless entreaties of the priest and their next of kin.

Even so, Murder risks going to sea. Night contemplates him at length. Soon she can see nothing more than the supernatural glow of his soft blue dolman. Soon, becoming aware of the first light of day, she slowly returns to her subterranean abode: her arms to the mines of France, her legs to Baikal, her body to California and her head to the Cape. The human ants respect the gigantic fragments of this delicate body and continue their labours to enlarge these palaces of darkness while the still youthful poet going to school sees negro archangels with eight red wings slowly ascending towards the sun. The labourer to whom he points them out says that it is the dew evaporating, though he himself, aware of decisive mysteries to come, falls to his knees beside a bush and meditates at length. Eventually he imagines that he is a hunter in Africa, in a soft blue dolman, galloping across the Sahara in the always forlorn hope of finding the adorable throat which must be slashed with a single stroke of his sword.

And while all this is happening, the distorted sun takes the shape of an hourglass and turns over. The poet tells himself again how much he would like to kiss a pouting little mouth, he tells himself much else besides.

The wheat ripens.

The black archangels descend from the sun.

Midnight, the murderous hour.

✳

A balloon drifted with the wind, taking on the appearance of — or so it seemed to me — in turn a poppy, a hand and a sword, although it is more than likely that the driver of the express train in which I was sitting, a thoughtful man whose profession frequently required him to distinguish between varying shapes and sizes, might have been able to enlighten me.

In any case, the cause of our disagreement soon disappeared. Despite the signals which were exchanged between the balloonists and the passengers, the train and the spherical shape went off in different directions, the former retaining the memory of a vertiginous roundness, the latter that of a trail of smoke. My gaze wandered across the peaceful plain over which pouting streams careered in search of the tall poplars which an industrialist had ordered to be felled and exported to Great Britain, a country which still venerates hangings; my eyes soon came to rest on a pink marble wall at the foot of which was sprawled a woman naked and murdered. The striking shape of her mouth, despite the paleness of my eyes and a distance of more than ten kilometres between us, indicated that her head had been humming with love and that rather than succumbing to the perfect embrace, the velvety drone of poetry had found it preferable to destroy the hive, kill the swarm of thoughts and the beautiful, tenuous queen bee with her pink fingers. The express continued on its way, preceded sometimes by the snow-plough of anxiety, sometimes the headlight of metaphysics, sometimes by a flock of golden pheasants, the messengers of madness. Spherical balloons still crossed my field of vision. My gaze still came to rest on walls of pink marble, but never again would balloonists or murdered women give my frightened soul that feeling of a vast plain, carefully cultivated and empty of human beings, under a violet sky during the chronometer's eternal hour.

O! Unlucky man! It would have been better to have gone up with the smoke as high as the rotundity of the airship or to have thrown yourself out the door and to have pitched up at the bloody body at the foot of the wall of pink marble across the fields and marshes.

Silence! Silence!

✳

A stupid accident almost turned the voyage of the balloon into a catastrophe. A spider which had hidden itself in the basket gave the balloonists such a fright that they almost leaped out into space. Fortunately, the insect decided to drop itself down suspended on its thread and the peasants, lured far from the barns where the threshing of the wheat made a dull sound with an inexpressible echo of love, were for some time able to contemplate this bizarre contraption carried by the winds of chance towards an unknown palace which, in place of an anchor, allowed this fearsome animal with enormous eyes, hairy legs and an ivory white belly to hang there, swaying dizzily at every movement of the balloon as if working some strange clock in the florid style fashionable at the time of Louis XV on which the half-undressed hours rotate around a globe.

Two travellers who met somewhere beyond the coast shouted to them with the help of a megaphone that they had never seen — or not until then at any rate despite numerous peregrinations to the four corners — any boats anchored with the help of captive squids held fast by a triple ring welded to a strong chain. But the balloonists, that is to say, the red archangel Raphael and the white archangel Raphael, both of whom were wearing the full uniform of café waiters, did not hear the astonished shrieks of overwhelmed humanity rising up towards them. At nightfall, the clouds wove them a most desirable shroud from the rough skins of camels.

Since then, the sky-blue boarding-school has been awoken every night by the aimless promenade of two waiters, one red and the other white. Ill omen!

Little girls, you will all die virgins!

✳

The train was crossing a marshy plain at the bottom of whose ponds successive suns had deposited a little of their transitory brilliance, the intangible moon had crinkled the grass-covered earth, and the distant stars had crystallised the edges of the marsh thistles which, as everyone knows, are violet-coloured. But the moon, the stars and the sun are common accessories and I shall not waste precious time describing them. The engine-driver was terrified that he had just "jumped" the fifth signal and that a disaster was now bound to occur at kilometre 178, which was marked by a milestone in the form of a truncated cone and a headstone commemorating the death at this spot on 17 July 1913 of a pilot named Jean de MARAIS, a death that his name had foretold. However, the fair-haired virgin and the yellow woman, with whose exploits we are already familiar, were busy working out complicated calculations at the foot of a poplar tree with the single intention of learning whether the engine-driver of the train negligently hurtling towards a telescoping rich in the loss of human life was your lover or my lover or her lover or their lover. While this was going on, the red star appeared above the poplar. At one of the doors in the sleeping compartment, another woman dressed in pink appeared and shouted: "I am the queen of accidents. My bouncing breasts, my arms, my taut stomach, my eyes, I have reddened them all in the most diverse calamities. On one occasion, I recall that at the very moment the water was about to fill the mouth of a shipwrecked man he nicknamed me FUNERAL and kissed me savagely. I have retained the mark of his bite out of pride… and ever since I have carried dust on my boots and the memories of men at the back of my eyes. The unutterable anxiety in which desire is entwined twists about you, as befits all lovers of a single night. I wend my way over the plain where the violet thistles are suggestive of bloody lechery and dragonflies, seeing a sister in each of my pupils, surround me with hummings. I am the queen of accidents. I preside over your encounters, tormented lovers and mistresses who torture their previous lover's memory. I am the queen of accidents. My mouth, like a piano, harbours transparent sounds and, when I allow it to speak, no one can resist the spontaneous sparkle of my red gums and my little, my neat little incisors."

*

Women's teeth are such pretty things that one should only see them in dreams or at the moment of death. It is the time of night when delicate jaws fasten on our gobs, O poets! Do not forget that a train, having jumped all the signals, is careering towards kilometre 178 and that, at night, our dreams, on the march for many a long year, have been delayed by two naked women talking at the foot of a poplar. Just as truly as we were contained in the first woman, our dreams were contained in the first dream. Ever since birth, we have been seeking one night to walk together side by side, even if only for a moment in time. Our age is infinity and infinity demands that the meeting, the coincidence, takes place today in a railway compartment hurtling towards disaster. Lock us in together, O poets! The invisible door opens on to countryside and an organ, yes an organ, rises up from the marsh. The fingers of the blonde woman, which I notice for the first time are webbed, ring out on it a joyful hymn. A wedding march of our reflections left behind in the mirror when the woman we ought to have met and never will comes to admire herself in it. A wedding march of hands severed as an ex-voto when death, offering us its basket full of violets, agrees again to read our horoscope. At the sound of the organ, the hangar doors open and release with a throbbing noise voluminous dirigibles into the open sky.

Awoken from his sleep, the pilot buried at kilometre 178 throws the points thirty seconds before the express arrives and aims them at the moon. The train goes by with its hellish din. It casts a shadow over our satellite and disappears like the song of the liner's engineer heard by mistake on the radio in the middle of a town in the South of France. The fair-haired virgin takes out a needle and sews a tiny purse full of freshly pulled teeth. She throws it at the fleeing stars and the sky henceforth assumes the appearance of a set of enormous and delightful woman's jaws. The same woman who will look into this mirror an hour after me. The pilot goes back to sleep and says: "I've got plenty of time to waste." The red star, the red star, the red star will fade at sunrise.

It was a very calm summer's night over a marsh.

A clock struck 1, 2, 3.

Beautiful blonde with the red lips!

✳

The king of a small negro tribe in the South Sea Islands finds on the beach a golden sceptre which had slipped from the imbecilic hands of a northern monarch and was washed up on the shore by the capricious tides. He picks it up with difficulty and returns to his capital lost among the leaves and creepers. A historian working in his study in Paris on the life and death of King Karl starts out for the peaceful spa resort where the woman he loves and who loves him is waiting, seventeen years younger than himself. In his suitcase, however, a nightingale tries on all his suits and decides that they are very well made. A storm breaks. The negro king implores the protection of his idols, the historian goes to sleep, the nightingale sings and wakes the historian.

Ridiculous events, but there is no qualifier for Destiny. Destiny leads the historian by his frock-coat, the negro king by his sceptre and the nightingale by its plumage. Thunder falls on the sceptre and kills the king; the jewel of regalia is covered by mud; the historian wants to silence the nightingale, shouts, bursts a blood vessel and dies, and his nephew inherits a suitcase containing a nightingale. Immediately taken with its bright colours, he brings it back to life in the hollow of his hand and installs the modest inheritance he has received from his historian uncle in his simple room. Then he sets off for a peaceful spa where he meets a woman of his own age. (Is he not seventeen years younger than his uncle?) They fall in love and one day take each other in his Spartan room in front of the singing nightingale. When *he* gets up, *she* is dead. He provides her with an honourable burial. But the smell, the smell of death remains. He consults books for the secret of this perfume: they do not reveal it to him. The nightingale reminds him of the South Sea Islands. They leave. They arrive on the island of the king who was struck by lightning. He walks over the mud where the sceptre of King Karl lies and continues on his way. He does not find the perfume, but bananas. He sets up a stall and makes a fortune. He returns to France where he is received in the best society. One day he gives his nightingale to a woman who introduces him to her husband:

"Monsieur Georges Dubusc, you know, the nephew of the Monsieur Dubusc who wrote that charming biography of King Karl."

The nightingale sings in its cage. For his trouble, he is given the name of Arthur.

＊

This is the story of three flowerpots in a window to which the midnight shadows lend the sinister appearance of a theatre in the lower depths of paradise at the moment when, the elect being asleep in their white beds, the clouds give themselves a treat by assuming human shape and dancing, much to the alarm of the empty heavens which three decorators coat afresh with black enamel in order to demonstrate the terrible resuscitation of thunder and lightning in God's green chamois-leather gloved hands. This is the story of a love letter lost by the postman at the corner of Rue Montmartre and Rue Montorgueil whose non-appearance draws dark rings round the eyes of a little sixteen-year-old girl in a garret while her desperate lover, waiting in vain for a reply, frequents the dance-halls where he gets to know an Argentinean woman who involves him in her love life, her fatal destiny, and her suicide. This is the story of a sculptor who suddenly discovers, while burrowing in red clay, that his roughing-chisel has the same shape as a murderer's knife and that, from the point of view of moral nobility, it is equally legitimate to throw living forms into silence and skeletal rigidity as to endow inanimate matter with a semblance of originality. He slips out through the streets and cul-de-sacs which are crossed, every morning, by the little orphans dedicated to the Virgin Mary and clothed in light blue on their way to hear mass supervised by a blonde nun who conceals dreadful secrets, six stretcher-bearers carrying three corpses, under her coif, and if they raise their eyes before going into Sainte-Eustache, they will notice three pots of geraniums in an attic window. The organs may send the healthy lions of contemplation prowling about them, the incense blights the yellow flowers in the English garden of mysticism, all to no effect: they will continue to dream their dream of the preceding night, particularly the whistle of the express heard with a start towards two o'clock in the morning.

Hidden amongst the poor, a postman will direct his thoughts towards God. He will ask the saints forgotten since the sunny days of his first communion the reason why he should be pursued by an intense feeling of guilt every time an envelope passes through his hands addressed in violet ink to a young girl on the Rue Montorgueil, an envelope which he invariably hands to the concierge who replies "Deceased" without him ever being able to fix it in his memory despite the black funeral hangings surmounted by the letter D in silver which decorated the porch one morning in February. He and the blonde nun will exchange holy water without deriving any more consolation than to hope for accidental drowning in a river squeezed between two asphalted quays, in a river still echoing with the sound of the fall of a body, that of a sculptor bearing in his heart the voluminous weight of a statue modelled on the Greek, with a slight Egyptian influence.

Wretched, wretched lives! As for me, I'm in love with the Argentinean woman. She dances between the rustle of the lights and the sparkle of her dress. Her body is flexible. She dances. She has slender hands.

Argentine woman, lead me to your light! If you brush the candles of the poor with the tip of your finger, they will burst into flames; you will breathe upon the eyes of men I am jealous of, and they will close. Argentine woman! Take me to the white jetty and the beautiful, the fabulous country of light.

❋

Thanks to the attentions of a woman we love, sleep clothes itself in our body just like a handsome snake which — while the sun, the creepers, the mosquitoes and the unpleasant smell of the rotting mangroves in a shallow swamp jar the nerves of the sand-coloured lionesses — slowly dresses itself in its shiny new skin, a new skin for a new year, identical to those touching calendars which book-keepers change on the walls of their offices every 2 January (because the 1st is a bank holiday) and which bear witness by their obtuse presence to the illusory mathematical unfolding of eternity before a procession of conquerors theatrically ranged before funeral monuments on which a stone angel tilts an urn of tears over a truncated column of historical characters on the point of death in the presence of a historian, of symmetrical battles and treaties being signed with peacocks' feathers by plenipotentiaries in full regalia in sparkling rooms, sleep, I repeat, clothes itself in our body while the woman we love who brought it to our bed is astounded by the funereal change that has overtaken our features, by the relative rigidity of our members and by our apparent indifference to the words which usually make us more dreamy than tall lamp-posts in deserted avenues at the onset of darkness. The woman gets up and sits pensively at the window where our dream follows her while the deserted street echoes from time to time with the dusty passage of motor-taxis and the languid footfall of a policeman on his beat. For a moment her white silhouette hovers in the air on a level with the third floor, and a young nocturnal rambler struck by this apparition, and imagining it to be the fall of a shooting star, articulates aloud his dearest wish: to sleep in a rocking-chair on a terrace.

It is two o'clock in the morning. It is sleep and his boisterous retinue of motley horses. The woman we love leads an orphanage of little girls dressed in sky-blue along the paths of a dark wood. An alert musician collects, thanks to his extraordinarily acute hearing, the different sounds made by keys turning in locks and dashes off one of the most beautiful compositions imaginable.

Tomorrow, the woman we love will dance to his refrain.

The bedroom door opens: the red archangel Raphael comes in followed by the white archangel Raphael.

It is sleep, it is sleep and his boisterous train of sandy lions and automobiles.

It is sleep.

＊

"Here lies he whose words assumed the shape of enormous northern flowers and who held in his strong arms that wild and deranged mistress, the woman as red as Red and coral which is, in fact, blue but which because of its tortuous shape has been endowed by poetic profundity with this colour which is known to excite bulls."

What a strange epitaph, I thought to myself, how very strange. But who can predict the sublime irony of those who turn their wills into objects of shame for their families and make a laughing-stock of their own memory. I could easily picture the amazement of the stone-mason on receiving his instructions to engrave this mysterious sentence on a block of granite torn from some rocky promontory and hewn into the shape of a parallelepiped rather than that of a plinth... Glory be to you, O granite! Covered in sharp edges as you are, to you the maritime gods expose their humid sexes, pell-mell with enormous fish and ships in distress, you are resplendent in your magnificent horror, and the pilgrim, the hermit and the sailor regard your jagged summit, which is like a tooth, a claw or a tusk in terms of shape but only at the moment the spume breaks in terms of colour, without an inkling as to the mathematical precision your future form will take with its eight ledges and eight rectangular dihedral angles, if we make no mention of perspective, wondering whether nature could have blessed you with a more beautiful role even allowing for the pink stain on your pinnacle which they would have been unable to decide whether it were blood, the fugitive sun, or coral which is, in fact, blue but becomes red through poetic profundity, that sturdy mistress, that savage woman who lingers over the baiting of bulls whom the fury of the oceans and the squids of your native region could not have frightened, while I myself know that the red stain on your summit gives you the appearance, O granite, of the most beautiful breast!

But, O granite, do not mourn your terrible majesty at the foot of the cliffs. Today, carefully carved as you are, and slumbering in this cemetery, a paper-weight holding down a body which has perhaps been turned into paper thanks to the use of putrid matter in the fabrication of that article, perhaps even the paper on which I am writing this eulogy, you assume the most majestically serene air by your association with the deceased who wished to carry away into silence even his name, a silence which extends to his very identity, and offers to the modest neighbourhood the dying echoes of a terrible peal of satanic laughter.

Paris, April 1924

NOTES

Although the title *Deuil pour deuil* may be translated literally as *Mourning for Mourning*, Desnos's original contains a pun on the expression *œil pour œil, dent pour dent*: an eye for an eye and a tooth for a tooth.

1. Bishop, preacher and theoretician (1627-1704), author of a classic statement concerning the divine right of kings.

2. Family of French executioners.

For a complete listing of all titles available from Atlas Press
and the London Institute of 'Pataphysics see our online catalogue at:
www.atlaspress.co.uk
To receive automatic notification of new publications
sign on to the emailing list at this website.
Atlas Press, 27 Old Gloucester st., London WC1N 3XX